I0717209

SPECIAL EDITION COVER

BEAUTIFULLY BROKEN

JOCELYNE SOTO

JOCELYNE SOTO

Copyright © 2021 by Jocelyne Soto.
All rights reserved.

Cover Design by Bee at Bitter Sage Designs
Edited by My Brother's Editor
This is a work of fiction. Names, characters, places, and incidents either are the product of the author's imagination or are used fictitiously. Any resemblance to actual persons, living or dead, events, or locales is entirely coincidental.
All rights reserved. No part of this book may be reproduced or used in any manner without written permission of the copyright owner except for the use of quotations in a book review. For more information, address: info@jocelynesoto.com.
Special Edition Published May, 2022

Special Edition Paperback ISBN: 978-1-956430-10-3
Special Edition Hardcover ISBN: 978-1-956430-11-0

BEAUTIFULLY BROKEN

BEAUTIFULLY BROKEN

EVERYONE HAS A BROKEN PIECE EATING AT THEM.
Some are just better at hiding that broken piece than others. I'm
the type of person that hides everything she feels.
At least, I try to.
There are moments where I just want to let the broken piece take
me away, so I don't have to live with the guilt anymore.
But when an old face comes into my life, I try my hardest to keep
my broken pieces away from him. I try my hardest to not let my
broken self show.
It was working. I was doing it. Until I gave in and shattered every-
thing.
I want to give this man in my life, everything that I have.
I want to open up to him, give him my heart.
But I doubt he wants to be with someone that is so broken like
me.

JOCELYNE SOTO

Never forget that you are loved. No matter what.

JOCELYNE SOTO

AUTHOR'S NOTE

This story touches on issues of alcoholism and
may contain triggers.
If you would like more information on these
triggers, please follow the QR code below.

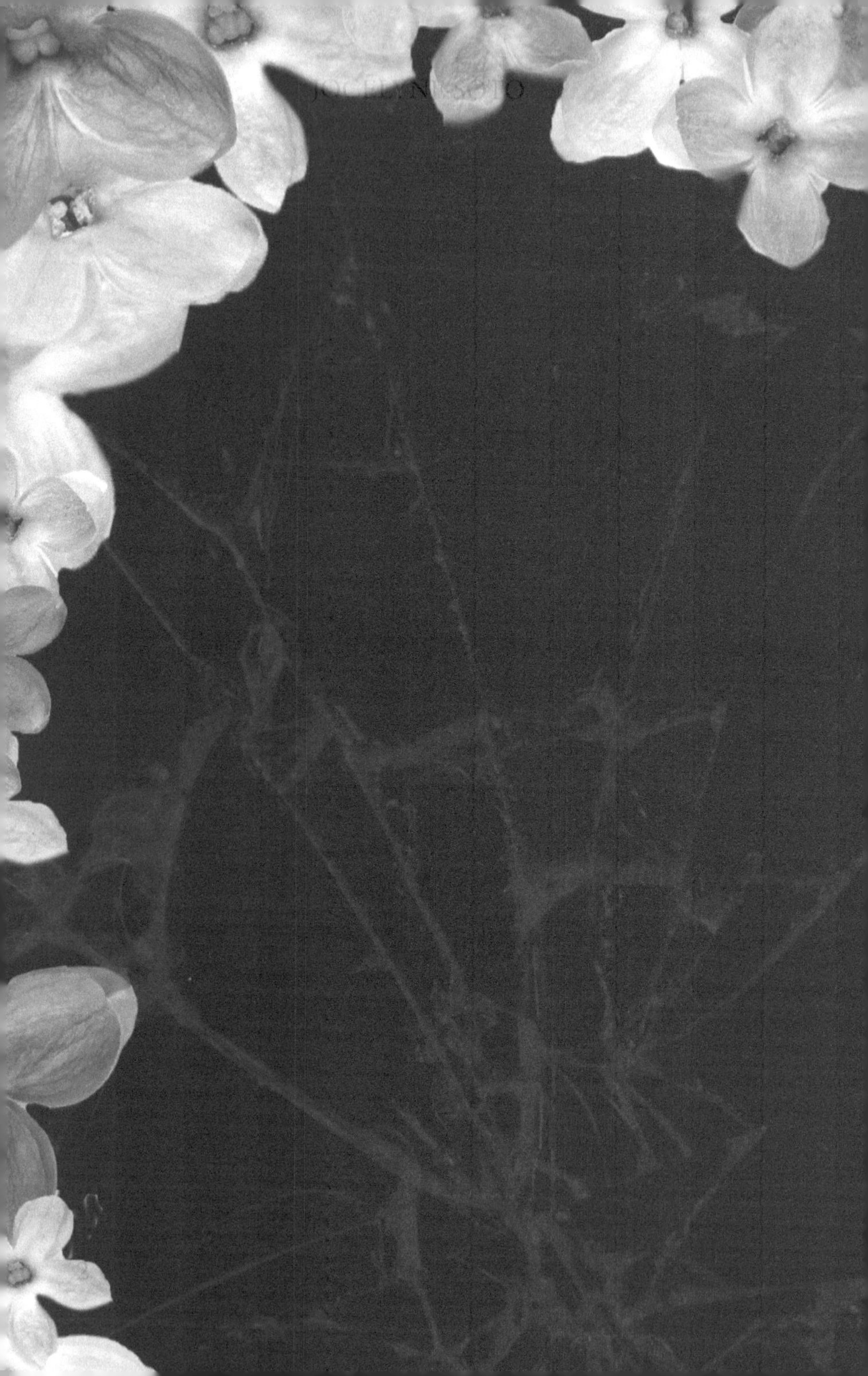

PROLOGUE

Jordan

Everyone has a darkness within them. Some individuals are just better than others at hiding it. I would say one of those people. I know how to hide the darkness that's within me.

I hide everything from every new person I meet. My life has darkness and sadness that will probably never go away. I go through days where I don't know if the darkness is going to suck me in and take over every cell in my body.

Today is one of these days.

A day where the darkness is threatening to suck me in and a part of me want to let it.

I was supposed to do a simple task. One that was supposed to take me fifteen minutes, tops. Then the darkness took over. My mind clouded up and I did the one thing I was terrified of doing. I put the lives of two important people in my life at risk.

People that have been there for me through everything, that have told me to get a hand on things, to stop throw my life away. Now it's too late. The bright red and blue lights are proof of that.

There is a numbness running through my body.

I feel like I can't breathe.

The ambulance took them and all I could do was stand there while the medics checked me out. If anything happens to either of them, I don't know what I would do.

I don't know if I would be able to survive.

It broke me when I saw the firefighters extract the back seat passenger, it felt like my world was exploding and there was nothing I could do to stop it. I kept begging for God to keep him alive. Keep him alive and take me in his place if needed be.

I will not be able to live in a world that he isn't in. Not only did I destroy my life, I destroyed his. He will never recover from this. And if he does, he will never forgive me. His trust and love for me is most likely gone.

I did this.

I can never undo it.

"Jordan?" A police officer says my name, I turn to face him. His face is full of concern but also disappointment. A face that I'm sure I will be seeing a lot of when word gets out about what I've done. "I need you to come with me."

I just stand there, not moving towards the police officer. I feel tears running down my face and after a long minute, I acknowledge him and make my way to where he is standing.

He cuffs me, reads me my rights and walks me over to his patrol car.

As he gets in the driver's seat and drives me to the station, I look at the aftermath. I see the car and how unrecognizable it looks. I see the tires up in the air, when they should be in the ground. I see glass shattered everywhere.

I catch a glimpse of the back seat, where he sat, the destroyed metal from where the firefighters took him out of the car. That sight is what breaks me.

The rest of the ride to the station, I sob.

I did this. I will never be forgiven, and I don't want to be.

He needs to make it, they both do, but he matters most. I already lost two people in my short lifetime. No way in hell will I be able to continue to live if I lose him too.

Please God, please don't take him away from me.

Please. I beg you.

CHAPTER ONE

If I could punch myself in the face right about now, or in the balls for that matter, I would.

Why would I resort to that sort of violence towards myself?

Because transferring to a different university during the second half of my third year might have been a stupid decision.

At least that's what I keep telling myself after driving over twelve hours from Chicago to Durham, North Carolina. I was perfectly fine at Northwestern, perfectly fine. there was no reason to move to another state. But Duke has always been the dream, so when an opportunity came up, I applied and I got in.

Arriving at Duke was supposed to be a glorious moment. Yet, with all the shit that I have gone through in the last couple of weeks, that feeling has been diluted.

The excitement isn't all at one hundred percent. It's more at like a forty five.

Now after twelve hours, here I am, in Durham, sitting in the driveway of the house that I will be calling home for the next year and a half.

And why am I sitting in the driveway you may ask?

Well, because I'm an idiot and decided to drive straight with only one piss stop in hour six. Now, I don't have the energy to open my eyes, let alone move or get out of the car.

I look at the cars parked in front of me, and try to picture the people currently living in the house. I'm supposed to be living with three other guys.

From the looks of things, one comes from money given the fancy Range Rover staring back at me. Then there's a Honda Civic that only looks like a few years old, must be a sensible guy and then there is an old Mustang that looks like it has been restored recently, I guess the third guy is a car guy. I wonder if I can distinguish which car belongs to who when I walk in without asking.

Might as well get in there and find out.

I grab my backpack from the front seat, I'll come back for the rest of my stuff later and make my way to the door and knock. When the door opens, I'm met with a pink haired girl.

Pretty.

But not what I was expecting. Did I come to the wrong house?

"Can I help you?" The pink haired beauty questions, with curiosity showing all over her face. Like I said cute but not really my type.

"Um." I look around trying to find the house number but I come up short. "Yeah, I'm looking for Carter Matthews? I'm the new roommate?" Why does everything I say sound like a question?

The pink haired girl nods and opens the door wider. I guess I do have the right house.

"Carter!" the girl yells into the house, and a guy that looks like the school quarterback comes out of somewhere. Hundred bucks he's the owner of the Range Rover.

"Hey. Mason, right?" The guy that I'm assuming is Carter extends his hand to me, which I take and give him a firm handshake.

"Yeah, nice to finally meet you," I say to him. Over winter break, I found a listing for a house a few minutes from campus that was looking for a fourth roommate. It was within my price range, so I reached out and thankfully it was still available, given that I waited until the last possible moment to look for a place to live.

We've kept in contact in the weeks since, but it was nothing more than pleasantries. I'm sure if we were women, we would have exchanged pictures or something.

"Yeah, same. Come meet the rest of the guys, and then I will show you to your room. You already met Lucy, she's here all the time," Carter waves at the pink haired girl.

"I'm not here all the time, I do leave." Lucy rolls her eyes at him.

"You sleep, eat and shower here. When exactly do you leave?"

"When you're not here," Lucy sticks out her tongue at him and walks toward the living room.

"I give her crap but in all honesty if she wasn't here all the time, I doubt this house would ever be clean," he says, leading me to the living room.

There are two guys sitting on the couch facing the TV, playing Madden on a Xbox. Lucy situates herself between the two of them, laying down, putting her head on one guy's lap and her feet on the lap of the other. The guy that has her head on his lap, strokes her hair back. Whereas the guy with her feet, pushes her off.

Not a weird dynamic at all.

"These are our other two roommates, Damon." Carter points to the guy stroking Lucy's hair. "And Gabe." Carter points to the guy who pushed Lucy's feet off. They both wave, without taking their eyes off the TV. "Damon is Lucy's boyfriend and Gabe is her brother." Carter says to me quietly.

That makes more sense. Defiantly wasn't think something completely different.

Carter shows me the rest of the house, and by the time that we make it upstairs, I'm speechless at the mere size of it. It's fucking huge. No way in hell would you find this type of house in Chicago.

"You get the master," he says as he guides me to a closed door at the end of the hall.

Well damn, I wasn't expecting that.

"Why?" I ask as I drop my backpack on the bare bed. This room is pretty nice. It's spacious and has a walk-in closet and a massive bathroom attached to it.

"All the other rooms are pretty spacious. My room also has a bathroom, and Gabe's and Damon's have that Jack and Jill thing. When the last guy moved out, none of us felt the need to move, so you get the reward," Carter gives me a blunt nod, like it's a done deal.

"I'm not complaining," I look around the room. The shit I can do with this space.

"We were going to order pizza, we can eat and then help you bring up all your stuff." I turn and Carter is at the door, pointing downstairs.

"Yeah, sounds good." I give him a nod. Never did I think that I would get roommates that were so accommodating. My roommates at Northwestern weren't anywhere near this level, and we were teammates.

We head back downstairs where Gabe and Damon seem to have finished their game of Madden and are now watching TV.

"Hey man," Gabe waves from where he is sitting on the couch once I touch the last step. He gets up from his spot and comes over and greets. "I'm Gabe."

"Mason," I say shaking his hand.

"This moody bastard is Damon." Gabe points to his

friend.

"Cut the 'moody bastard' shit. Your sister has no problem with it," he gives Gabe a wink, insinuating something else. Now I have the mental picture of the two fucking. Great.

Gabe gags at his words, "My sister has a lot more problems when it comes to you."

"Ignore them. They've been fighting like that since we were kids, even more when D and Lucy started dating." Carter starts moving past me and Gabe, heading for the kitchen.

"You guys have been friends since you were kids?" I ask, following behind him.

I can't help but think about how I just moved into a house and have a feeling that I'm about to be treated like an outsider. Hopefully that isn't the case, I already feel like an outsider, no need to feel more.

Carter nods. "Yeah, we all lived in Wilmington, met on the army base more than a few years back. We connected over the fact that we're army brats. Stayed close ever since," he says taking a water bottle from the fridge and offering one to me. I shake my head.

"All your parents are in the army?"

"Yeah, pretty much." He takes a drink of the water before he answers, "My dad is a colonel and Damon's mom is a captain. Gabe and Lilly lost their dad a few years back in Iraq and their mom is currently in Germany."

Fuck.

When it comes to knowing people in the military, I know of one person. A family friend that has been in my life for a few years. He's currently stationed in Hawaii, so I don't really stress about it.

I don't know how I'd be able to handle one of my parents being in the army though. Let alone have one of them die while serving. It's not something I can wrap my head around.

Luckily, Lucy comes barreling into the kitchen, putting our attention on her, making it easier for me not to say something stupid concerning military parents.

"Have you heard from Jordan?" she asks Carter. He nods at her. "Yeah, talked to her this morning. She said that she was coming up tonight."

Lucy lets out a sigh. "She said that two days ago."

"I know, but she said that she had to take care of something with Alana, and that tonight was a for sure thing, she bought her bus ticket and everything." Carter gives her a small smile.

"She better, or we're going to drive to Wilmington ourselves and drag her ass back here." Lucy gives him a curt nod and heads back to the living room.

I know I shouldn't put myself in other people's business but I can't help it.

"Who's Jordan?" I sound like a nosy creep. If I get kicked out of the house, I will definitely know why.

The second that I say the name, Carter's facial expression changes. It becomes harder, like he's pissed off that I said this girls name or something, but it quickly morphs back to one of boredom.

"Another friend from back home," he says, not giving me anything else before he takes another drink of his water, ending the conversation.

I just nod, not wanting to put my foot farther in my mouth. Apparently asking about whoever Jordan is was the wrong move and makes Carter a little pissy.

We end up ordering that pizza that was mentioned and watching movies the rest of the night.

As the night goes on, I can't help but think about this Jordan girl.

Why did Carter's face shift when I asked about her?

More importantly, why do I care so much about someone I never met before?

She's probably his girlfriend or something and he's just a possessive asshole.

Takes one to know one.

I really need to figure out a way to make my mind shut the fuck up.

CHAPTER TWO

"Mommy, can I go play with the girl over there?" I ask my mom by pulling on her leg. She's talking to her grown up friends and I rather go play than listen to them talk about boring stuff.

She bends down to my level and looks over at who I'm talking about. She gives me a smile, "Of course, honey. I think she would like that. Go ask her."

I nod at her and head over to the girl who is wearing a pink princess dress and black Converse.

"Can I play with you?" I ask her, kneeling in the sandbox next to her. She looks up at me and gives me a smile.

"Do you know how to build a sandcastle without the ocean? I can't make it stay up." She looks like she wants to push the big mountain of sand away and stomp on it.

"I've never been to the ocean, but I can try," I tell her. My grandma and grandpa live by the ocean but I've never seen it.

"Okay, let's make it big," she says and starts building a sand hill.

"I'm Mason." I look up at her. Her eyes are the

color of chocolate bars.
      "I'm Dani."

* * *

I'm jolted awake.

It takes me a quick second to realize that I'm in my new room at Duke.

What the hell was that?

Was it a dream? If it was, it felt like it was clear as day. Like what had happened in the dream, actually happened in real life. Weird part is, I don't remember that ever happening.

When did I ever build a sandcastle with a strange girl?

Shaking the dream out of my head, I reach for my phone and check the time.

Six thirty.

You would think that after driving so many hours yesterday, my body would let me sleep, but I guess it's still on a baseball schedule.

Baseball.

The sport that for most of my life, was the one thing that kept me going. The one thing that I had that made me who I was.

Baseball was one of the reasons I decided to transfer to Duke. Not only was it a great school, but their baseball program was topnotch. Everyone who is everyone in the college baseball world, knew Duke Baseball was the program that made major leaguers.

Then I had to go and hurt my pitching arm while doing drills at practice a few months ago and the dream of playing Duke baseball went out the window.

My elbow was torn, and the only way I would ever

be able to throw at the level again was if I had Tommy-John surgery. It wasn't a guarantee, so I decided to end my career and move on.

Being able to attend Duke to finish my degree is a blessing but at the same time a big kick in the balls. I part of me still wants to play and I can't help but think about the what ifs.

Throwing the covers off my body, I put on some shorts and head down stairs to find something to eat.
A run should be the first thing that I do this morning, but I don't have the motivation to do it.

Rubbing my eyes as I make my way downstairs. The house is silent, telling me that everyone is still asleep and not crazy to start their day this early.

I walk into the kitchen and when I look up, I'm taken aback.

Standing right in front of me, reaching up to get a coffee mug, is a girl with wild brown hair, in a t-shirt and panties.

How do I know she is wearing panties? Well because her shirt has ridden up and her ass, a delectable one at that, is on full display. Only a scrap of material covering her up, a very thing scrap of material.

Fuck.

If I wasn't the man that I was, I would be going up to her and placing my hands all up on her backside. Feeling how smooth her skin might be, and how she would fill up my hands.

I shake my head.

Those are not thoughts I should be having when I don't   have much fabric myself covering my lower extremities. Especially when it comes to a strange girl, I have more respect for women than the shit flowing through my mind right now.

I knock on the wall to announce my presence.

"Why the hell are you knocking?" The girl turns and when she sees me, her eyes go wide, startling herself, dropping the mug on the floor. Ultimately breaking the mug.

"Fuck," she leans down and starts to pick up all the broken ceramic. I head over to help her clean up.

"I didn't mean to scare you. I didn't know anyone else was awake," Or that there was a strange girl in the kitchen.

"It's fine," she mutters, looking up at me, keeping her concentration on the floor.

I wonder if maybe she might be Gabe or Carter's girl. If she is, I'm going to feel like an ass for thinking about hers.

"I'm Mason. The new roommate," I introduce myself when all the broken pieces are picked up.
She just nods at my introduction, still not even looking in my direction.

Okay, then.

She gets up and throws away the broken mug and just goes back to making her coffee. And I for some reason go back to staring at her ass. It's a nice ass.

You're such a creep.

My concentration is broken when someone clears their throat. I turn and find Gabe standing at the kitchen entrance with an eyebrow raised.

I feel embarrassment covering my face.

"Well good morning sunshines what's with all the noise at this lovely hour?" Gabe gives me a smirk before heading over to where the mystery girl is and grabs a cup of coffee for himself.

"I broke a cup," Mystery girl lets out.

Gabe nods, "When did you get in? I didn't hear the chime go off," he changes the subject, turning his attention back to her.

My guess if he didn't know she was here, then she must be Carter's girlfriend.

"Around two," she sighs, still not looking up.

"Where did you sleep? Since the master is taken." For some reason, and this may just be me, but I'm finding this whole interaction a little weird.

Also, if she were Carter's girlfriend, wouldn't she be sleeping with him? Why would she sleep in what is now my room?

"The couch. I wasn't going to make Carter sleep on the floor."

I'm so confused right now. Is she not Carter's girl-friend? If she isn't, then who is she? And why isn't   Gabe as affected by this girl standing in the kitchen in just panties and a T-shirt as I am?

"Cool beans, I'm going to head back to bed because I'm not a lunatic like you two and like waking up early."

Gabe leaves the kitchen, leaving an awkward air in his wake.

I watch the girl as she watches the floor, trying very hard to not look at me. She's beautiful, her hair is in wild waves over her shoulders and down her back. She has legs for days and from what I can see she has a body worth drooling over. Curves for days, and about five-five.

Without a doubt, I bet that she has beautiful eyes too. Part of me wishes that I was able to see them when I was helping her with the broken mug, but she kept her eyes down and I wasn't able to get a good look.

"So," I kill the silence that's in the room. I don't know why, but I want to know who this girl is. Maybe I'm just being stupid and should have followed Gabe upstairs.

When I speak, she finally looks up at me and I'm met straight on with a set of beautiful brown eyes that look like they can suck at your soul. They're dark and deep and if I stare into them long enough, I will be sucked in.

"So?" she asks, raising an eyebrow at me.

"I didn't get your name," I throw out there, just trying to keep her talking, keep hearing her voice. Her voice has a crispiness to it but also a smoothness to it, if that makes sense.

"That's because I didn't say it." Feisty, I like it. She shakes her head and lets out a sigh. "I'm Jordan."

So, this is Jordan.

Now I can see why Carter was defensive about her last night when I asked. He said they were friends but maybe he wants to be more, and I wouldn't blame him. This girl is a freaking knockout.

"Nice to meet you," My words earn me a nod. I don't say anything more. Why make it any more awkward than it already is?

Moving around her, I grab a mug and serve myself some coffee. As I move, she doesn't do anything but drink her coffee and keep her eyes on the ground.

I   'm about to ask how her coffee is but the words that leave my mouth are completely different.

"I guess I'll see you later," I say instead, heading back upstairs. Before I leave the kitchen though, I turn around again and catch her looking at me. I can't help but smirk a little.

"Nice panties by the way."

Her eyes go wide and I realize what I just said.

Oh fuck.

Why would I say that? Am I looking to get my ass kicked?

"I-I, that's not what, I didn't mean," my mind feeling all jumbled up. "I'm just going to go upstairs and pour this hot coffee all over my head."

What the actual fuck is wrong with me?

I run upstairs and before I hit the top step, I hear a laugh coming from the kitchen.

Glad someone finds my mortification funny.

That isn't what has me smiling as I walk back into my room. It's the fact that I made the mystery girl laugh.

Panty comment and all.

One point for me, I guess.

CHAPTER THREE

Throughout the years, I have done everything in my power to learn new ways to control my emotions. It's the only way I'm able to take my life where I want it to go and not down a dark hole like it has before.

I know how to control them. Well, that is until something takes me by surprise and I don't know what to fucking do.

That's what happened this morning.

Carter told me about two weeks ago that they found a new roommate and that he was going to move in soon.

I just brushed it off. Whoever they moved into their house had nothing to do with me, I didn't really care about a new roommate. As long as he wasn't an asshole, I was good.

Even though it wasn't of any importance to me, I should have asked for a name. A name, a description, something so that I wouldn't have been shocked when I saw him at the entrance of the kitchen.

For a quick second, I thought he was just a hallucination but I quickly realized that it wasn't. There really was a guy standing a few feet away from me, in basketball shorts and no shirt.

I knew who he was right away.

He might have been older and a lot more manly with facial hair and muscles all over his body, but I knew him. I knew his name, his age, everything.

It was like the part of my past that I wanted to ignore, was jumping out in front of me, asking for attention.

I knew he wouldn't remember me, I watched how his eyes held no recognition. It was so long ago when we first met, I've become an entirely different person in the years since. But just because he didn't remember me, doesn't mean I didn't remember him.

He was the first boy I ever had a crush on, and that's not something that a girl easily forgets. Not even with all the dark shit that has happened in her life.

Mason Hawke, oh how you have grown into a man.

A every hot, mouthwatering man.

This is definitely not something that I thought I would have to deal with during my third year of college.

I can't believe that he's here, but honestly I'm not surprised given that his dad went to school almost twenty years ago.

But what are the odds that he would not only be at the same school as me but also be my friends' new roommate?

When he went back upstairs, I collected myself the best I could, especially at six in the morning, changed and headed back to my dorm.

The only reason I was up that early was because I couldn't sleep. The bus from Wilmington to Durham was late, so I arrived back to campus around one in the morning. When I went to my dorm and saw that it was empty, Lucy probably spending the night with Damon, so I walked over here.

I didn't want to be alone, because being alone brings out the demons and I really didn't want to deal with those at one in the morning.

I don't want to deal with them period.

So I came to the one place where I wouldn't be alone. Carter, Gabe, Damon and Lucy would be there and I would be able to get at least a few hours of sleep. I used my key and got settled on the couch for the night.

I waited for sleep to take over but it never came. My eyes were closed but my brain was awake, contemplating every little thing.

The nights that I can't sleep are the ones that I dread with a passion. Those are the nights that my past comes to haunt me the most.

Instead of fighting for sleep, I turned on the TV and curled myself onto the couch.

Now, I'm getting my books for the start of the semester and I'm a walking zombie. No amount of ice coffee is going to make me feel more alive.

"You look like shit," a male voice says behind me. A voice that I could recognize anywhere.

Carter.

My best friend.

He and I met when we were around nine. My dad had just gotten re-stationed to a base out in Wilmington, so my mom packed up me and my brothers, leaving Texas behind, and headed for North Carolina.

Carter was in my fourth grade class and when I introduced myself and said my dad was in the army he screamed out that his was in the army too and we bonded.

Throughout the years, he has become my confidant,

my shoulder to lean on, the older brother that looked out for me. We have a close relationship, in a very platonic kind of way. A sister and brother relationship of sorts, and it will always be that way.

Don't get me wrong, Carter is what people would call the all-American boy, and girls drool over him on a daily. It's just not for me.

I turn in the direction of his voice and see him a few feet away, dressed in his usual sweatpants and hoodie. The way he's dressed isn't what got my attention though.

No, my attention went straight to the male specimen standing next to him.

A mouthwatering specimen.

Again with the mouthwatering? Get your shit together Jordan. You are not in the mental capacity to go down that road.

Wait, did Carter say something?

"What?" I turn back to my best friend, who is looking at me with confusion.

"I said that you looked like shit." His blond brow lifts up as if he is asking me what is wrong with me.

"I didn't sleep very well." It's better to give Carter half-truths than to completely lie to him.

Carter's head bobs taking the textbooks that I have in my arms from me, "You should have taken my bed when I offered."

"I can carry those, you know." I say completely avoiding the bed question. Any other time, I would have taken him up on his offer, I have plenty of times before. But had I walked into his room last night, he would have interrogated me about shit I don't want to talk about. Shit that I wanted to avoid and well I wasn't up for a therapy session.

Carter just shrugs at my statement and balances the books in his arms.

"Have you met Mason?" Carter nods toward his new roommate standing next to him.

"We met this morning," Mason tells him, without taking his eyes off of me, a small smile playing at his lips.

He's taunting me, great.

"Really?" I can hear the question in Carter's voice. He's probably wondering how he didn't know this, maybe he thought I would text him or something. I don't have to tell him everything that happens in my life.

"Ah- huh." I feel a blush creeping up my neck, as I remember exactly what I was wearing for that kitchen encounter.

I don't like the feeling of pajama bottoms touching my legs while I sleep, okay?

So panties are my go-to. It's just that sometimes I forget that I'm wearing underwear that doesn't necessary cover anything. Like this morning.

"Yeah, imagine my surprise when I walked into the kitchen and saw a beautiful girl in next to nothing reaching up for a coffee cup," he says with a smirk on his face and I have no idea if he is teasing me or flirting.

I'm going with teasing.

But that isn't what my mind is concentrating on at the moment. It's the fact that he called me beautiful.
I'm so rattled by that little statement that I don't notice Carter's raised eyebrows questioning my actions.

"You couldn't put on pants?" His question takes me out of my head.

Did I mention that Carter is like the big protective brother that I didn't want? Especially when it comes to guys. It gets annoying at times.

"I didn't know anyone was even awake or that he had moved in. So I went about my merry way and didn't think about putting on pants." I'm comfortable around my three guy friends enough to not wear pants or shorts when I sleep.

Carter doesn't care, Gabe will never see me in that light and Damon is so enamored with Lucy that he will never look at another girl.

Mason on the other hand, might be a different story.

"I didn't mind it," Mason says ending the intense face-off between me and Carter. Again, I can't tell if he is trying to tease me or actually flirting.

My blush grows a little more and my best friend turns to glare at his new roommate.

Before this whole situation becomes any more awkward, I take my books from Carter. I need to get away from Mason Hawke before I say something stupid.

"It was nice talking to you two ladies, but I have to go. I've got shit to do." Turning my back to them, I head to register to check out.

Once I'm out of the bookstore, thankfully Carter and Mason didn't follow me out, I head to my dorm room.

When I walk into the room, it is quiet, since Lucy is most likely with Damon. I settle onto my bed   a f t e r placing my books on my desk.

should unpack the clothes that I took with me back home during winter break but instead I pull up my phone and call my mother's best friend.

"Hi sweetheart, I was wondering when you were going to call," she answers the phone after the second ring.

"Why didn't you tell me he was coming here?" I ask. Phoebe Hawke had been my mother's best friend since they were in high school. The woman that was like a sister to her and is like an aunt to me and my brothers. She was a major part of our lives when were just babies, not so much now since I haven't seen much of her in the last ten years, but we talk occasionally.

Phoebe lets out a sigh, "I knew there was a chance of you running into him, but Duke is a big school. I didn't think it would be so quick."

"He's my friends' new roommate," I state.

"Of course he is." She lets out a sigh, like she isn't surprised by this news at all. "I'm guessing he didn't recognize you?"

I shake my head even though she can't see me, "No, he didn't."

Maybe him not recognizing me is a good thing.

He could get to know the person that I am now and not the person that I turned into all those years ago.

CHAPTER FOUR

You know how some college students despise morning classes? Well for me, I hate night classes with a passion. They ruin too many plans, and after a while they can become a hassle.

I try to stay away from night classes as much as possible. But when you transfer to a new school for spring semester at the last minute, that isn't an easy option.

If you want to know why I waited a month before the semester started to accept my transfer that story will have to come another day. Not because I don't want to tell it, but because there is a brunette beauty a few feet in front of me that just grabbed my attention.

Jordan walks by me, not giving me any attention and walks into one of the nearby classrooms. Checking the class schedule I have on my phone, I smile when I see it's the same classroom I should be heading into.

I guess I have luck on my side.

In the week or so since I moved here, I haven't spent a whole lot of time with Jordan. She has come over to the house almost every single day, but she doesn't say much. She mostly keeps to herself and only contributes to the conversation when required.

At first, I thought that it was because she wasn't comfortable around me just yet. So, I asked Gabe one day and he told me that she has always been that way.   H   e said that Jordan was a shy and quiet person, and add her shit on top of that, she has a right too.

I wanted to ask what "shit" he was referring to, but I kept my mouth shut. It's not my place to know that about her. If one day we grow close and she wants to tell me, she can.

After that conversation, I saw her in a different light. I saw her as a girl that just wanted to be with her friends and get a degree, so I decided that I'm making it my mission to be her friend. Who doesn't need more friends?

I know I sure as hell do, given that my only friends here are my roommates. The friends from back home dropped me faster than a bag of shit.

Following her into the classroom, I watch as she walks down the auditorium style stairs and heads to the fourth row before taking a seat.

Interesting, I would have figured her for a back row kind of girl.

Not thinking much of it, I walk over to where she is sitting and thankfully the chair next to her is still open. I pull it out and take a seat, right away Jordan's attention is on me, her brown eyes are wide with surprise.

"Hey, you don't mind if I sit here, do you?" I give her a smile. She stares at me for a solid minute with those wide eyes of hers, before she shakes her head and takes an AirPod out of her ear.

"What are you doing here?" she asks, looking around slightly as if she is looking for one of my roommates to pop out.

"Human Memory, right?" I say to her as I take my laptop out of my backpack and place it on the table getting ready for class to start.

"Um," she sounds confused by my statement.

"Yeah. You're a psychology major?"

It's not the first time someone has questioned my choice in major. Shoot, even my father asked me about it.

Given that I'm an athlete and have played baseball my whole life, people automatically assume that I'm studying something in the sport science department.   That's the furthest thing from the truth actually.

I like learning about humans and why they may think a certain way or do the things they do. So I went with psychology when it came to choosing a major. It's what called to me from a long list of subjects.

I nod my response to her. "I didn't know that you were one too," I say that like I've actually had a conversation with her about this subject.

She looks at me for a few seconds, before she looks to the front of the room. "Sometimes the things that captivate you the most come from the things that you have experienced."

Cryptic.

It makes me wonder what experience she's talking about.

Are they the same ones that Gabe mentioned?

The professor walks in and starts talking before we can continue the conversation any further.

Through the explanation of the syllabus, I'm very aware of just how close Jordan is to me. Her thigh is mere inches from mine and my hand itches to place itself on it.

I have no idea why this girl that I hardly know is affecting me so much. In the week since I have met her, I have found myself staring at her, wanting to hear her laugh, wanting to touch her. Everything.

No girl has affected me in this way, and because of that, it might be why I think it's best to be her friend. If this girl has this effect on me now, imagine what that effect would be like if I actually expressed my feelings. If I actually told her that I wanted to touch her thigh and hear her speak.

By the time that the professor is excusing the class, I spent more time studying Jordan than listening to what he said.

Once she has her things packed up, Jordan stands up, and starts walking out of class, not saying a word to me. As if I didn't spend a whole class sitting next to her.

I quickly put my laptop away and race to follow her out. No way is she leaving without me, I didn't get my fill of her just yet.

"   Any plans?" I ask, opening the door for her, waving her through. She whispers a quick "thanks" before giving me a small smile and walking through.

"Not really, I was just going to get something to eat before heading back to my dorm."

"You're not heading to the house?" She's been at the house every day since I moved in, she has even slept there a few nights, here being there feels normal.

She shakes her head. "I have a few things to get in order that I have been neglecting. Besides, I'm sure everyone has plans or something to do."

"I don't." I realize how quickly I said that when I see her trying to keep in a laugh.

"Are you trying to make plans with me?" she asks through a chuckle, and I can't help but to laugh with her.

"Maybe I am. How do you feel about grabbing some pizza or something?" For some reason that I cannot explain, I'm really hoping that she says yes.

She rolls her lips trying to fight a smile and gives me a small nod. "Yeah why not? I'm starving."

"Cool." I have become a doofus around this girl.

Once we are in my car, she directs me to a pizza place that is about fifteen minutes away from campus. The whole drive and even after we order our food, Jordan is quiet. She only really talks when she was giving me directions or telling the cashier what toppings she wanted on the pizza.

Just so you know, she's one of those pineapple on pizza girls.

When we are situated at a table in the back, I finally decide to ask the questions that are sitting on the tip of my tongue.

"So, have you lived in North Carolina your whole life?" Not the best question, but I want to know everything about this girl.

She shakes her head. "Was born in California, but with my dad in the army, we moved around a lot and ended up in Texas. Finally we settled in Wilmington when I was about nine."

Huh, small world.

"Where in California were you born? My parents are from there and my grandparents still live there." I take a drink of my water, keeping my eyes on her face. I watch as she gets a weird expression but then it quickly forms into a small smile.

"Um, San Luis Obispo," she says her lips rolling into her mouth.

"Really? That's where my parents are from." California is big, and I half expected her to say one of the major cities or an obscure town I never heard of. Never the same town my parents grew up in.

"Strange coincidence," she mutters before taking a sip of her water, like she wants to change the subject.

"Any brothers or sisters?" I ask after the waitress places our pizza in front of us and walks away.

"Two brothers," she mumbles as she takes a piece of the pizza. "You?"

"One sister, she's sixteen."

"My younger brother is the same age." She takes a bite of her pizza.

"And your other brother?"

She stops mid bite, shock covers her face, like she didn't expect me to ask about her other brother.

Jordan chews her pizza, with her eyes on the table. I guess her older brother is a sore subject. She swallows.

"Three years older," She finally says, still not meeting my gaze. A harsh note in her voice.

Okay, her older brother is a sore topic. Next subject.

We spent the rest of the time eating our pizza and talking about random things. She tells me about her relationship with my roommates and how their friendships all started. She speaks about her dad and how he is currently stationed in Afghanistan and is set to come home sometime this year, if all things go well. There is a tinge of hope in her eyes when she tells me how he is one of the last of only a couple thousand troops left in the country. Hopefully things work out and she able to have her dad home sooner rather than later.

She asks me about my family and my life and I tell her anything she wants to know. I speak about life as a big brother and how life was in Chicago. I tell her about baseball and how I ended up getting hurt and falling into a depression after being told I can no longer play and deciding not to go forth with the surgery that would ultimately fix my pitching arm.

"I'm sorry that you can't play anymore. It must really suck to do something for years and then have it taken away like that."

I bob my head, "It does, but the injury made me realize that there was more to life than just baseball. I was never going to make it big, that I understood, but it was still a big part of who I am today."

"That's a good way of looking at things," she says before taking a bite of her crust. I nod at her again.
We are quiet for a few minutes before I get the courage to ask her another question that has been on my mind.

"So, you talked about your dad. What about your mom?" I ask cautiously. Maybe talking about her mother is also one of those sore topics like her older brother is.

Jordan surprises me though. Her eyes do go wide but they don't fill with shock or even anger like they did earlier. No, this time they fill with sadness and maybe appreciation that I'm asking about her mother? I don't know but it's not what I thought I would get. This girl keeps surprising me.

She takes a deep breath, "She passed away when I was ten."

"Fuck. I'm sorry. How did she pass if you don't mind me asking?" What the fuck is wrong with me? I shouldn't be asking her about this. I should just give her my condolences and move on.

I hear an audible swallow before she answers my question, "I don't mind." She stops and takes a deep breath, "Stage-four breast cancer. They found it too late and she didn't want to get any treatment."

"I'm sorry."

"Yeah, me too." She gives me a small smile before she goes back to eating her pizza.

There's something about this girl that makes me want to go to her and wrap my arms around her and tell her that everything is going to be okay. But of course I don't.

We finish our pizza and our drinks and soon we are heading back to my car and I'm driving her to her dorm.

When dropping her off, I tell her that it was nice getting to know her and I threw out there that I hope we can be good friends one day. She gave me a smile and said that she would like that.

Yup, I friend zoned myself. It's not something I wanted to do, but I don't think either one of us is in the right mindset to be anything else. Besides we just met, shouldn't I get to know this girl first before pursuing her?

* * *

There are tears streaming down her face, but she isn't shaking like her dad is. She is sitting there next to her father, looking at her mom's casket, with tears running down her face.

I want to go to her but I know my mom won't let me, she'd want me to stay by her side.

Turning to my parents, I see that they are also cry-

ing and shaking just like her dad is and I want to do every-thing in my power to make it stop for them. They look like they are in pain.

I hate seeing them like this.

My eyes turn back to Dani. I watch as she gets up from her seat next to her dad and heads down the hall to where the bathrooms are.

Without asking my mom, I get up from my own seat and follow Dani down the hall. I follow her as she walks to a door and stands in front of it, not reaching to open it. She just stands there, like she's waiting for it to swing open by someone on the other side.

I walk over to her and stand at her side, not saying a word.

In the years that we have known each other, Dani and I have become friends. She's funny and likes to play things like ninja and baseball with me.

We stand there in silence, looking at the door. The only sound is coming from the living room. I turn slightly to look at Dani and she has more tears sliding down her face.

I take her hand in mine and grip it tightly.

"I'm sorry about your mom, Dani," I whisper.

She turns slowly to face me, sniffing in the process. Her big brown eyes are filled with tears and her face forms into a small smile.

"Yeah, me too."

* * *

It's like cold sweat running down my back.

This is the second time that I have been woken up by a dream like this. It seemed so vivid. So real.

As I try to calm down my breathing, I can't help but think that I've seen those tear filled eyes somewhere recently, but I have no idea where.

Dani.

She was the little girl that I had a dream about a few weeks ago. The one that I was building a sandcastle with. How didn't her name click the first time I had a dream about her?

Why is it only clicking now?

I haven't thought about Dani in years. She was a friend that was a part of my life when I was younger but in the years since that funeral, I haven't seen her. She was a girl that was a part of my life one day, but not the next. I think I nearly broke me leaving her after that funeral. In the years since I last saw her, I would have the occasional thought about her, something random would pop into my head but nothing like this.

Never in my dreams. Never revisiting aspect of our time together.

The thing that is tripping me out, is if I haven't seen this girl in years and only occasionally thought about her, why am I dreaming about her now?

And why do those brown eyes seem so familiar to me now?

CHAPTER FIVE

"How is school going?" my stepmother, Alana, asks.

Alana came into my life about ten months after my mom died. My dad met her at a bar after one night of drinking. According to her, she was there with a few friends when a guy came up to her and started touching her inappropriately. My dad played hero and stepped in to stop what could have ended badly. Apparently they clicked after that encounter because they ended up spending the rest of the night together talking and they ended up exchanging numbers. They started dating and Alana started coming around the house and meeting me and my brothers.

I hated her at the beginning.

I hated her so much that I even begged my dad to not marry her when he told me he wanted to propose. I didn't need her in my life. She wasn't good enough to take my mom's place.

He pulled me into a tight hug that day and told me that my mother would always be in his heart and that he would always love her. He told me that Alana made him forget about the pain that he was feeling and made him believe in love again, that she made him happy.

There was no way I could being mad at that, no way could I take away his happiness. So they got married, two years after my mother had passed away.

After their wedding, that's when I started diving through a dark hole. A dark hole that to this day still haunts me. A hole that lead to drinking to feel something, drinking to forget things and getting high to dream of a better life.

The combination of those two things became an addiction that I held near and dear to my heart and wouldn't let anyone pull it away from me. I hid it and nobody questioned me about it. Nobody saw what I was doing behind closed doors. Nobody saw how I was destroying myself when I was left alone.

Not my dad, or my new stepmom. Not my teachers or my friends parents'. Nobody that really needed to see.

The only people that saw it, were the people that were doing it right next to me, but they never saw how broken I was. How I let the broken pieces take over.

The person that I thought would be by my side to help me when I needed it most, left without a backward glance. Having him leave was just like a domino effect, everything just kept breaking more and more.

"Jordan!" Alana's voice breaks me out of my mental spiral.

"Um, sorry." I shake my head and try to think about what she just asked. "What did you say?"

"I asked how school was going," she says in her stern mom voice. Alana and my dad never had kids of their own, but she treats me and my younger brother like we are hers and sometimes her mom voice comes out to play.

A voice that I know all too well.

Alana has been the mother figure that I needed after

my mom died and I'm thankful for her.

Even when I was a complete bitch to her , she has been there for me even on that faithful day all those years ago. The day that I broke beyond repair.

Not the time to think about that, Jordan.

Right.

"It's okay. Classes are slowly starting to get in the groove of things. Things should be getting crazy soon." I tell her as I try to fold the laundry that is currently taking over my bed at the moment.

"Do you think that you can handle the course load? I don't want you to overwork yourself." I don't deserve a stepmom like Alana, especially not after all the shit I put her through.

"Yeah, I got a handle on things." I smile at her even though she can't see me.

"Good. I'm glad that things are going okay." She lets out a sigh of relief. I wonder how she would be okay if I had decided to go to school out of state.

"Yeah. How's Dylan?" My little brother is in his senior year of high school, and when I was leaving home a few weeks ago, he was excited about the college offers he was getting to play basketball.

"Oh you know, exercising every single day because he says he needs to be bulkier. Oh and after you left, he threw out all the food that was in the fridge and had us go to the store to get all organic crap." I can hear the head shakes and eye rolls from here.

I can't help but let a laugh escape, "Well, if all that helps him choose Duke, then I'm all for it."

"You and I both know that he's going to choose Duke. He's been talking about their program since he was twelve,"

Alana says, and my mind goes in a different direction for a second.

Yeah, and it almost got taken away from him.

"Have you talked to Dad?" I change the subject because I don't want to think about how things could have been different for my brother.

"I did, this morning. He said that he was going to give you a call tonight if he had a chance. It looks like he might be home before May if everything goes well." I can't help but smile at her words.

My dad is finally coming home.

He's been in Afghanistan for the last seven months. This is supposed to be his last tour, so he says, and he will start his retirement process.

Daniel Garza has been in the army since he enlisted at the age of eighteen. My mom was pregnant with my older brother. They had just gotten married and needed a steady income. Enlisting seemed like the only option to him.

Throughout the years he has climbed up the ranks and earned honors that to any civilian, would be amazing. To him, it's just about getting the job done. I can't wait to have him home permanently.

Alana talks for a few more minutes and then tells me that she has to go to the grocery store. After hanging up with her, and I finish folding my laundry, I let my mind drift.

I let myself think about how my father is about to retire from the army, yet my older brother has years to go.

My older brother.

My brother that was my savior at one point. The person I depended on more than anyone else. The person that protected me.

BEAUTIFULLY BROKEN

He was my everything, until he wasn't.

* * *

A bang wakes me up. I don't need to check the time to know that it's the middle of the night. I sit up and wait to see if I hear anything else, but the house goes back to being silent.

No way my dad or Alana didn't hear that bang. It was loud and I couldn't have been the only one that heard it.

After sitting here on my bed, not even hearing a door open, I decided to go investigate the noise myself. Opening my door, everything is dark and the only light I see is coming from under my brother's door.

I bet he heard the bang.

Slowly, I walk over to his door and knock lightly before turning the knob and opening the door just enough to poke my head in.

My brother is sitting on the floor, leaning against his bed, with his head down between his knees.

He looks a lot younger than his fifteen years of age when he's like this. He looks like a scared little boy right now and all I want to do is make things better for him.

"Den?" I ask, and right away his head shoots up. His eyes are red, like he has been crying. I have never seen him cry, not even when our mom died.

He wipes at his eyes and gives me a sad smile. "What are you doing up so late?"

I walk into his room and close the door behind me, "I heard a noise, so I wanted to check what it was."

He nods, "Yeah, sorry, that was me. I dropped a

bottle," he says bowing his head once again.

"Bottle?" I go over and sit next to him, sitting crisscross applesauce.

Den sighs and grabs something from his other side and shows it to me. It takes me a second to realize what it is.

My eyes are wide when I turn to face him. "That's Dad's whiskey."

Our dad keeps his fancy alcohol looked up in a cabinet in his office. We aren't supposed to touch it, and I can't help but wonder how Den got his hands on it.

"It is." Den looks down at the bottle in his hands.

"What are you doing with it?" He's not old enough to drink, he's only fifteen. That bottle should be locked up where dad had it. If he finds Den with it, he's going to ground him for weeks.

"Drowning all the pain away," he tells me, still keeping his eyes on the bottle.

Pain. He's in pain.

"What kind of pain?" I wonder if it's the same pain that I'm experiencing. The one that has been there since we found out that Mom was sick. The one that got even stronger when she died and Dad got remarried.

"The kind that doesn't go away no matter how hard you try. The pain that keeps you up at night. The kind that you don't feel when you fall off your bike or break a bone. This is the type of pain that is inside of you, that you feel everywhere and you want it to go away so badly but it doesn't."

I listen to his words and digest them as best as I can.

The pain that he is explaining is everything that I'm feeling.

I wonder if I drink the whiskey if I won't feel the pain anymore.

"Can it take my pain away?" My brother's eyes grow wide at my question. He stares at me like he can't believe that I just asked what I did.

Den is silent for a long time before he lets out a sigh and opens the bottle, taking a drink before handing it to me.

"Just this once, and you don't tell anyone, ever, that we're doing this." His face is stern and to be honest a little scary.

"I promise." I take the bottle from him and study it. What is the amber liquid in the bottle going to taste like?

Am I going to like it?

There is only one way to find out.

With one final look at my brother, I take a drink from the bottle.

I took my first drink with my older brother next to me.

And no, it wasn't just that one time.

* * *

I still remember how that bottle of whiskey tasted on my tongue. It made me cringe but after a few more tries, I was able to get past the taste and swallow it down.

That fateful night happened almost ten years ago. I was thirteen, and Den was sixteen, and to this day I have not told a soul that it was my brother that let me have my first drink.

I'm not angry at him for not stopping himself from giving me that first drink.

I'm angry at him for everything that happened after that.

CHAPTER SIX

Her bottom lip is between her teeth. Her hair is a wavy curtain covering half of her face.

I just want to reach over and brush it away, so I can see her eyes move as she reads from the page in front of her. Maybe even release her bottom lip and take it between my teeth, just to get a little taste of her.

My jeans are getting slightly tighter under my zipper. Fuck. I shouldn't be thinking about my friend this way. Especially not when she is sitting right in front of me and my roommates are in the other room.

Because that is what Jordan is to me, a friend. Maybe that is all that she will ever be.

In the almost month since we met, Jordan and I have become friends, somewhat close but friends nonetheless. I'm not going to jeopardize our friendship by drooling over her. No matter how much I want to.

I clear my throat, trying to clear my head from the thoughts of Jordan as much as I can.

Shifting my eyes from the beautiful brunette next to me, I try to concentrate on the assignment.

Jordan and I are currently studying for our first test that we have in our one shared class. Got to love professors that give tests so close to the start of the semester.

As much as I try to concentrate on the work that I need to do, my eyes keep drifting back to Jordan.

There is something about this girl that makes me want to throw everything that I have learned about girls out the window.

Sure, I've had girlfriends, and girls that were more than friends, and more than enough one night stands. But why do I feel this gravitational pull to Jordan? What makes her different?

"So, no boyfriend?" I ask, breaking the silence in the kitchen. The words are out of my mouth before I can stop myself.

Did I really ask her that? What the actual fuck is my problem? Why do I keep blurting out questions around this girl?

Is that even a question that a friend could ask, right?

Jordan's eyes slowly move from her textbook to me. They are a little wide like she can't believe that I just asked her that.

Yeah, me and you both.

I can't get a read of her face so I backtrack, "Sorry, I don't know what possessed me to ask that. Ignore it." I wave my hand at her, trying to make my eyes concentrate on my own textbooks. Hopefully a hole will open up and the earth will swallow me whole.

I hear a sweet chuckle coming from her, so I build up the courage to look up and see that she is fighting letting out a full blown laugh.

Giving me a smile, she speaks, "It's okay, I get the curiosity. No, no boyfriend."

I nod, not meeting her gaze. From just seeing them interact, I came to the conclusion early on that her relationship with Carter and Gabe is a strictly platonic one. She actually has a brother/sister relationship with all my roommates. So it made me curious to know if a girl like Jordan had a boyfriend back home.

Now I have my answer.

"Or a girlfriend," she says, prompting my attention to go back to her face.

"Yeah, me neither." I say to her and she grants me a bright smile, as she holds in a laugh, which just makes me want to let out a laugh myself.

I'm about to say something else but Damon comes into the kitchen grunting, looking like he's in pain. Given the way he's limping, I going to take a wild guess and say that the dude is hurt.

"Why are you limping?" Jordan asks him. I guess I'm not the only one that noticed the limp. It might be just me but I hear a hint of worry in her voice.

Damon shrugs and heads to the fridge. "Landed wrong during practice. Nothing too bad." He takes out a water bottle from the fridge, no cares in the world.

Damon is on Duke's baseball team, it's something that we had bonded over since I moved in. Had I not gotten hurt, we would have been teammates as well as roommates.

"But you're limping." The worry that coated Jordan's voice a few seconds ago becomes more prominent. She's definitely worried about him.

Damon notices too because he turns to her and gives her a reassuring smile, "It's just a sprain, nothing to worry about. I have a session with the trainer later and then after a few days I will be good as new. Nothing to worry about."

I watch as he gives her another smile and before he leaves the kitchen, he walks over to her and places a kiss on her hair. He's reassuring her, telling her not to worry about his injury.

Why is Jordan so worried about Damon being hurt? The expression that comes across her face is not only worry, but also pain and maybe even some guilt.

Am I missing something?

Damon leaves the kitchen and joins Carter and Gabe in the living room. Once we are left in the kitchen alone, I keep my eyes on Jordan.

She is looking at the space that was just occupied by Damon. Her eyes are blank, like she has gone to a different place. The expression that she was wearing earlier is gone and in its place it's something that I can't decipher.

"Jordan," I say to her, trying to get her out of whatever place her mind is.

I don't even get a blink when I call out her name.

I wave a hand in front of her face and still nothing. There is a blink now, but it's just an automatic motion.

"Jordan." I practically yell. Finally her head jerks and her eyes close, possibly ridding of the haze that was like an overlay on them.

"What?" she asks, her eyebrows bunching up in confusion.

"Are you okay?" I really want to know what just happened.

"Yeah," she says and then then takes a pause before giving her head a shake, "Yeah, I'm okay." she says with a lot more confidence.

"Are you sure?" That wasn't a normal reaction that someone should have.

She nods and gives me a smile, one that doesn't reach her eyes. "Yeah, I'm sure."

For some reason, I don't believe her.

* * *

After studying most of the afternoon, Jordan and I decided to call it quits and order pizza and soon she was leaving to head back to her dorm. I wanted to ask her to stay, because I wasn't ready to be away from her, but I didn't. So, I watched as she left the house with Lucy at her side and told myself that this was all my idea.

It's currently after midnight and I'm in my room watching some stupid crime show on my laptop. I'm not even paying attention, my mind is too preoccupied by a certain brunette that is across campus at the moment.

Even when she is not in front of me, she occupies my fucking mind.

My phone starts to ring, taking my mind off of her. I look at the time on the top corner of my laptop and see that it's close to one in the morning.

Who the hell is calling right now?

I reach for my phone that is on my nightstand and check the caller ID.

Of course. This man doesn't understand the concept of time zones.

"Don't you know what time it is? I could have been sleeping." I say instead of a greeting.

"Oh, you know that sleeping is for pussies," he says with a laugh.

Aiden Hall is a family friend that has taken the place of an older brother to me of sorts. This is the family friends that's in the army and is currently stationed in Oahu. So he is six hours behind North Carolina time.

He has been a part of my life since I was fifteen. It was during a time that I needed someone my own age to help me figure out a path I wanted for my life.

My family and I were in California for a few weeks one summer and Aiden came by to see my parents. He had just enlisted and he and I bonded. He is three years older and sometimes acts like a prick, but hey he's a friend. Can't help but have a sweet spot for the guy.

"Yeah, yeah. What's up? I haven't heard from you in a few weeks." In the years that we have known each other, we've talked at least once every few weeks. With him being in the army, and constantly moving to different places, it can be a little hard to keep in contact.

"Sorry about that. Shit got a little crazy for a bit but things have finally calmed down. How's Duke going?"

I scratch my head. "It's going good. Wish I was playing but there's nothing I could do about that. Other than that, it's a great school and my roommates are awesome. No complaints from me."

"Well, that's good. But man it would be awesome if you were playing for Duke."

Thanks for the fucking reminder.

"Yeah it would be," I basically mumble into the phone.

Aiden is silent for a few seconds before he asks, "Any girls grabbing your attention?"

I can't help but snort. Yeah, there's one certain girl, but for some reason I don't feel the need to tell him about Jordan. Not yet at least.

"No, no girls," I say to him.

"Good, you're only young once. Get as much pussy as

you can before settling down." This coming from a married man.

"And are you telling me from experience?" I smirk. Aiden used to be a manslut before he married his now wife. He and Sara, his wife, were a thing in high school or something but broke up, somehow they reconnected and are now married. The time between high school Sara and the Sara of now, Aiden went through women like kids go through crayons. Like I said, manslut.

"Something like that. Just don't make the same mistakes that I have."

I nod even though he can't see it. "I'll try not to."

We talk for a few more minutes before I hear Sara calling him in the background, calling him for dinner. He tells me that we should plan for him to come visit me soon and then hangs up.

Once my phone is back on my nightstand, I close my laptop and throw my head back on my pillow.

Maybe I should take Aiden's advice and get as much pussy as I can. Maybe then I would be able to get Jordan off of my mind.

But just thinking about Jordan has me all worked up. So much so that I'm sliding my hand into the front of my sweats and stroking myself as I think of her hand or mouth on me. Pleasuring me.

I continue to fuck my hand, picturing Jordan in front of me with those pouty lips of hers.

It's not long before her name is on my tongue and I'm exploding in my hand.

After I get cleaned up and in a new pair of sweats I realize there is a chance I may never get Jordan out of my head.

And I don't think I want to.

CHAPTER SEVEN

Jordan

"Are you sure Damon is okay?" The question comes out as I sit on my bed and Lucy is rummaging through the closet in our dorm room.

She came in this morning like a tornado from hell after her morning class, rambling on about needing something to wear.

It looks like the Captain is in town and taking Damon and Lucy to dinner. When it comes to Damon's mom, Lucy is always a nervous wreck. I don't know why, but she has been this way since high school. I think that it might be because Lucy has it in her head that Damon's mom might tell him that he could do better.

She won't, because the Captain loves Lucy, but yet she doesn't see that. She just sees the scary woman that the Captain can be and cowers in her presence.

"He's fine. It's just a sprain, the swelling and the limp will be gone by the end of the week." She voices as she throws yet another dress on my bed.

"But it's the leg" I start to say but Lucy pops her head out of the closet and gives me her death stare.

"Babe. He's fine. You have nothing to worry about. I

promise." Her eyes are filled with sincerity and I know that if it was worse, she would tell me.

When I saw Damon limping yesterday, my stomach dropped. So many scenarios popped into my head as to why he was limping. Each and every one of them made me more and more cynical.

I'm sure that paranoia will be there until I see it with my own eyes that the limp will go away.

The worry like obsession that comes with Damon getting hurt started a few years ago, when I destroyed everything and almost ruined his future.

Every time he gets hurt like this, the guilt takes over all over again. Just like it did all those years ago.

"Uh! Where is that dress?" Lucy yells out, taking me out of the dark turn that my mind was about to take.

"Maybe at the guys' house?" I offer. I don't even know what dress she's talking about. but given that she sleep there more than here, it's very possible that whatever she's looking for, it's there.

She pokes her head out again and gives me a confused look.

"Why would it be there?" Seriously?

"Because you practically live there? The only time you sleep here is when D is at away games."

When the five of us all got into Duke and decided to attend, the guys got the house and Lucy and I decided to live in the dorms. The guys offered for us to move in with them, but with all my emotional and mental shit I was going through, I decided it was best to live in the dorms.

Lucy and Damon had been together for a year before coming to Duke, so I thought she would take them up on the offer. She surprised me when she said that she wasn't ready for that step just yet. So she moved in with me.

We both spend most of our time at the guys' house, but I come back to my dorm most nights. Lucy does not.

"I spend nights here," she says with a smirk. I can't help but roll my eyes.

"I don't get why you just don't move in. You guys have been together for almost five years," I tell her as she abandons her place in the closet and comes to sit next to me on my bed.

"You know, we both could have moved in when the master was free. Then we would all be under the same roof," she wiggles her eyebrows.

"Yeah, no. I already have to deal with you and D making out all the time, I don't know if I'd be able to deal with it twenty four-seven." Seeing two people that you see as siblings practically eat each other is not a pretty sight.

"Why? Damon is hot, of course I can't keep my hands off of him. How you don't see him in that light is beyond me." She shakes her head.

"It's beyond me that *you* see him in that light." Don't get me wrong, Damon is good looking but he doesn't do anything for me. Neither does Carter or Gabe.

Their roommate, on the other hand, is a whole different story.

There is something about Mason that I gravitate toward. Maybe it's his broad shoulders or his growly voice, or maybe it's his hair that I want to run my fingers through.

He's not the first guy that I might have had feelings for, but for some reason the tingling sensation in my stomach is stronger when he's around.

A sensation that I don't want to go away. I like the feeling and if I'm being honest, if my life wasn't the shit hole that it is, then I would pursue it. It is a shithole and this Jordan doesn't deserve anything other than a friend.

"D is just so yummy. What's not to like?" she says in a dreamy tone and I fake gag. "Shut up." She shoves me and I can't help but laugh at her description of her boyfriend.

Our giggles die down and Lucy turns to face me. "Are you okay?"

I nod, not knowing what she's getting at.

"I mean, are. You. Okay?" She enunciates each word, trying to get her meaning through my thick skull.

She's worried about me. She has always worried about me and every so often, she asks me to open up to her, so that she knows that broken pieces within me aren't becoming even more shattered.

I let out a sigh and give her a small bow of my head, "I think so. I've been thinking about the past a lot these last couple of weeks though," I say, giving her a small smile.

"Why?" Her eyebrows furrow, eyes coating in worry.

I shrug, "Maybe it's because I went home for the holidays. Maybe it's something else. I think that's why I started to freak out when I saw Damon limping."

What I don't tell her is that the root cause of everything most likely has to do with Mason Hawke coming back into my life. And the whole not remembering that we met once upon a time.

"Have you…?" She trails off but I know what she is trying to get at.

Do I lie to her?

"I haven't done anything. I've thought about it, the urge has been there but it hasn't been very strong for me to go out and do it." I give her a sad smile.

Her face is now more worried than anything. I hate

that she is looking at me like this. It makes me feel like I'm going to break and she is just waiting for it to happen.

"Please tell me that you reached out to…" Again trailing off, it's as if she can't say the words.

I give her a nod. "I have, more than I would like to fucking say, but yeah. I've reached out."

Watching my best friend, the girl that has stood at my side even through some of my darkest days, and see her eyes go from worry to sadness. Soon, the corner of her eyes are being flooded with tears.

"Why are you crying?" I ask her, reaching for her hand and taking it in mine.

"Because you're twenty-one. This isn't something that you should be dealing with. You shouldn't have to be scared about this type of thing."

"Sometimes life has a fucked up way of writing certain paths. Mine isn't a normal one but it's mine and I have to step over every little rock or hole that's in my way. It's a challenge, but I have do it and I'm okay with that. You have to remember that I did this to myself."

Lucy keeps her eyes on me for a few seconds before that she nods and she scoots closer to me and wraps her arms around me.

I find it a little funny how I'm the one consoling her right now, but I'm okay with it.

It's nice to have Lucy like this. It's nice to have someone in my life that worries about me like this, that will stand by my side when I'm at my darkest.

Since there are those that will and have walked away from me when shit got tough.

CHAPTER EIGHT

The sound of metal hitting against the ball rings in my ear over and over again. It's a sound that I grew up around, a sound that has a calming effect on me. A sound that makes me wish that I was out in that field instead of sitting in the bleachers.

I watch as the guys on the field, the ones that would have been my teammates, practice play after play. I should be down there with them. There should be a glove in my hand and a ball in the other, sweat running down my face from the North Carolina heat. I should be doing all that, but I'm not.

"You know, if you didn't go and hurt your arm, you could have been out there." Damon's voice comes from somewhere in front of me. I turn and see that he's in his practice uniform, climbing up the stairs to, walking over to where I'm sitting.

"Shouldn't I tell you the same?" I throw back at him.

"Touché." He climbs one last step and sits down one row below me, leaning back, on placing his elbows on the bench next to me.

Damon is what some girls would call a bad boy, or a rebel, whichever, I have no fucking clue. He has this swagger to him that most guys would kill to have.

I say most because if you ask me, I have the same swagger.

"Why aren't you down there?" I jerk my head towards the field.

He shrugs. "A hairline fracture stops you from doing things like running and landing on your foot."

Fracture?

"Didn't you tell Jordan it was a sprain?" The conversation was over a week ago but I'm sure that I didn't imagine him saying the word sprain.

Damon shrugs again. "If I had told her the truth she would have freaked out even more. Me telling her that it was a sprain saved her from spiraling down the rabbit hole."

"How are you hiding a fracture in your leg?" Hairline fractures are small but they are a bitch when it comes to pain. You can't really walk and the injured is supposed to keep any pressure off of it for a few weeks.

"I have my ways." He turns to me and gives me a smirk that I'm sure makes Lucy crazy.

Turning back to watch the field, I watch the guys for a few minutes before I find myself asking a question that I shouldn't.

"What does you hurting your leg have anything to do with Jordan? Why does she care so much?"

These questions have been playing in my head all week. I still can't get the reaction Jordan got to seeing Damon limping into the kitchen out of my head. Why would she care so much about that? I understand that she is his friend and everything, but why would seeing him hurt, even something so small, affect her in any way?

And why the hell would he have to lie to her about

the extent of his injury?

There are so many things that don't make any sense about this situation. And if I'm being honest with myself, there are a lot of things that don't make sense with this girl.

Damon turns his vision back to the field, deep in thought. After what feels like forever, he lets out a sigh and speaks.

"The summer between my junior and senior year, I was in a car accident that almost took my leg from me. Somehow the doctors were able to save it with minimal damage. I had to do some rehab, but after a few months I was good as new and was able to be on the field come that spring."

Shit.

"Damn, but what does that have to do with Jordan?"

"Jordan and I were extremely close back then, like we spent most of our time together. In a platonic way, but still it was a lot. I guess her seeing me like that did something to her and now she is just worried if I so much as let out a groan when I get off the couch."

Again, he gives me a shrug, putting an end to the conversation. I feel like there is more to it, but I doubt he will tell me anything more. I bet if I ask Jordan, she wouldn't tell me either.

Damon and I go back to sitting in silence, watching his teammates practice. I wonder if he feels the same thing I do, the urge to run down to the field and play. By the look on his face, I would say that he does

We watch the rest of practice and when everyone is walking off the field, Damon turns to me. "You want to meet the guys?"

I shouldn't.

Meeting my would-be teammates would just mess with my head even more, but somehow I find myself nodding at Damon and following him to the field house.

Duke is a powerhouse of a school, one that really cares about their athletes. I know this the second I walk into the field house. Everything is state-of-the-art. Exercise equipment, locker rooms, showers. If this is what the baseball locker rooms look like, the basketball lockers have to be filled with opulence, because fuck, this place is nice.

I continue to follow Damon deeper into the field house until we make it to the locker room. Once there, it's like everyone knows of his presence and stops talking to hear what he has to say.

"Guys, this is Mason Hawke. The guy that would have been one of our starting pitchers." He claps me on my back giving me a curt nod in the process.

"I think starting pitcher is a little bit of a stretch," I throw out there with a smirk. All the guys laugh at my statement and one by one comes over to me and introduces themselves.

"You guys should come by the house tomorrow night, we are having a party for one of the sophomores," a guy that introduced himself as Ricky, says to me and Damon.

"Yeah, and D can bring his girlfriend and hot piece of ass roommate that she has." A guy next to Ricky says, before he licks his lips.

I don't know his name, but I don't give a shit. He's talking about Jordan, I know he is, and his words have me seeing red.

"What did you say?" I growl at him, ready to beat the shit out of him.

"Damon's girl has a roommate that I wouldn't mind

pounding my dick into once or twice. Get my hands on that beautiful ass." He gives me a wink and that's when I lose it.

My hands fist the collar of his shirt and slam him against the wall of lockers.

"Don't. Ever. Talk. About. Her. Like. That." I spit the words in his face. The asshole is just looking at me like I'm the crazy one.

"Calm your down friend," the douchelord says with a smirk. He thinks Damon is going to side with him, he should know better than that.

"I'm good. Want to know why?" Damon says, moving next to me and leaning in close to his teammate. "Because she's my family, and no one gets to disrespect my family."

D places a hand on my shoulder, silently telling me to let him go. Without taking my eyes off of douchelord, I slam him against the lockers one more time before letting him go.

"You know what?" Damon says, taking my attention from his "friend". "I think we will go to that party, that way Jesse here can apologize to Jordan himself." Damon pats Jesse's face a few times to drive a point.

Jesse doesn't say anything, just keeps looking at me and Damon with disgust. D gives him another pat on the cheek before he heads to his locker, and quickly grabs his things and nods to me to follow him out.

I flip Jesse off before I follow Damon out.

The walk to the parking lot does nothing to dissipate the anger I have bubbling inside of me. I want to go back into that locker room and punch the shit out of that fucker Jesse.

"I got to say, dude. I didn't think that you had it in you," Damon says with a low chuckle.

"He called Jordan a piece of ass," I say through my teeth. He can't be defending him.

"I heard him, and if he wasn't my teammate then I would have pounded his face into the wall. He's an asshole." D stops walking and turns to me. "Thanks for standing up for Jordan."

His face is sincere and filled with gratefulness. I don't know just how close Damon and Jordan are now that they are older, but I can see that he cares for her. He cares for her like a sister and he showed it in the locker room, he will protect her and stand by her side.

I nod. "She's my friend too."

He gives me a smirk. "Yeah, *friend*. You and I both know you want to be more than a *friend*."

Am I that obvious?

CHAPTER NINE

Sometimes I wish that I didn't live on a college campus. Or that I had skipped the whole college experience altogether. Not because I didn't want the education, but because everywhere you look there is temptation.

Temptation to skip class.

Temptation to experiment.

Temptation to drink, do drugs, anything that may make you feel included or to make you forget.

College for me is a temptation, one that I cannot escape and sometimes I don't want to.

My friends, who are more family than anything, know what my triggers are; they try to keep me from them as much as possible, and I love them for it. Sometimes though, they need to go and live their lives and enjoy themselves.

They shouldn't be suffering through boredom because of my stupid decisions.

"Are you sure?" Carter asks as he pulls his jacket over his shoulders, getting ready to head to the baseball house for a party.

I nod from my current place on the couch. "I'm sure. Go have fun. I will be here rewatching *The Dark Knight* for the millionth time." I know when not to put myself in situations that I will regret.

Carter looks at me, trying to find something that tells him that I'm lying, that I'm not okay about staying here by myself.

"Maybe I'll skip the party and stay here with you." He moves to take off the jacket that he just put on. Sometimes I hate the over protectiveness.

"Carter, I'm good. This isn't the first time I've stayed in this big house all by myself. I know where the emergency numbers are at and if I hear a strange noise, I will call 911." I give him a smirk. I'm being a smart-ass, but shit I'm twenty-one, I don't need a babysitter.

"Fine." He sighs, exasperated, fixing his jacket again. I can't help but laugh at him.

Footsteps sound as everyone else comes down the stairs, Damon, Lucy, Gabe and Mason coming to join the party of two.

"Why are you dressed like a hobo?" Lucy yells out when she hits the bottom step. Of course, her pink hair is done up to perfection and wearing a short dress that I'm sure Damon loves.

Compared to her, I am looking like a hobo. My hair is in a messy bun on top of my head, my glasses are on and I'm wearing sweatpants and one of Carter's hoodies. I look like a mess, and I wasn't regretting it, that is up until I made eye contact with Mason.

He gives me a smirk, one that I want to kiss off his face. Never did I think that a man could make a pair of dark washed jeans and a long sleeved Henley look so damn sexy.

I shake the thoughts of a mouthwatering Mason out of my head and answer Lucy.

"Because I have a date with Batman." I give her a serious face. Why else would I be dressed like this?

"Seriously?" she whines, and I'm sure that if she was still the girl she was in high school, she would be stomping her foot too.

"Sorry." I say taking a drink of the iced coffee I got on my way over here.

"I was going to find a hot baseball player for you to fuck."

I start choking on the liquid and coughing it up.

"Jesus," one of the guys says, and I can't decipher who because of the coughing fit taking over my body.

After a few seconds, I get the coughing under control, I look at my friend, giving her wide eyes.

"What? You need to get fucked, and who better to do it than a baseball player?" She shrugs and all the guys look at her.

Heat rises up my neck when Mason meets my gaze. I wouldn't mind sleeping with a baseball player, if *he* is said baseball player.

"Can we not talk about Jordan getting fucked? I rather not have that picture in my head." Gabe groans and makes his way to the door.

"Are you sure you'll be okay here by yourself?" Carter asks as Lucy and Damon follow her brother out.

I roll my eyes. "Oh my god, leave. I'm good." I point toward the door, making him leave. He's cutting into my precious Heath Ledger time with his over protectiveness.

"Fine, I'm leaving but if you need anything I'm a text away." I swear Carter is more of a father sometimes than a friend.

I raise my eyebrows at him and he holds his hand up

in defeat and walks out the door. The only one left is Mason.

"Are you going to convince me to go too?" I give him a smirk and he lets out a low chuckle. A low chuckle that has me pressing my thighs tighter together.

"Nah, but do you want the truth?" he says coming closer to me, a playful expression on his face.

"Of course," I breathe out as he comes closer and closer to me. I'm pretty sure I'm no longer breathing when he leans into my ear and speaks.

"I would rather stay here and watch a Batman movie with you than go to a party." Why do the simplest words have me all hot and bothered?

It may be just me being aware of his proximity but I swear I can feel his lips grazing the bottom of my ear.

Mason pulls back and gives me a smirk and a small wave before following everyone out the door and closing it behind him.

I let out a breath as soon as I hear the door click shut. I'm pretty sure that the crush I had on Mason when I was a kid has nothing on the crush I have on him now.

Especially since now I know how to use a vibrator to help with all the shit I feel when I'm around him.

* * *

Two hours into *Justice League*, the Snyder cut obviously, the front door opens and Carter and Mason walk in.

Picking up my phone, I see that it's close to one in the morning. They left around ten, I'm kind of surprised they are back so early.

"Where are the other three musketeers?" I ask when

Mason closes the door behind them and Carter comes to sit next to me.

"Gabe is still at the party and Damon and Lucy went back to your dorm." I scrunch up my nose at Carter's words. Great, if those two went back to the dorm, I'm going to have to sanitize everything tomorrow.

"I guess I'm sleeping here tonight," I let out, putting my attention back to the screen, vaguely aware of Mason coming over to sit on my other side.

Just breathe Jordan, the man is just sitting.

Yeah well, tell that to my erratic breathing.

"You can take my bed and I will take the couch," Carter offers.

I shrug. "I'm cool with the couch, besides it lets me finish watching the movie," I say not taking my eyes off of the screen, overly aware of how close Mason is to me.

"If you say so, I'm going to crash then." Carter lifts himself off the couch before turning to head for the stairs. "'Night guys."

I watch as Carter goes up the stairs with wide eyes. He's leaving me here alone with Mason. As my best friend, can't he see how much his new roommate has an effect on me?

"This movie is so much better than the theatrical cut." I turn to Mason and see that he has thrown an arm over the back of the couch and his legs are spread out, invading my space.

"It is. Long but it's worth it," I say, turning back to the TV.

"Wouldn't have pinned you for a DC girl, I for sure thought you would be all hot and bothered about Marvel," Mason says and I hear a smile in his tone. Sure enough, he has a grin taking over his face and his eyes or glistening.

"*Justice League* all the way. Don't get me wrong, I've watched all the Marvel movies, but they bore me and don't grab my attention as much as DC movies do. And let's be honest, DC makes better cartoons than Marvel does."

Oh my god, I can feel the nerd in me coming out.

"True." He gives me a sly grin, "I gotta ask, who's your favorite Batman?" An eyebrow raises to challenge me, and I just want to lick it.

Where did that come from? Since when am I into licking eyebrows?

I feel a blush creeping up my neck, but I avoid it and answer his question. "Christian Bale. Yours?"

"Michael Keaton."

"Fair choice, if you would have said Lego Batman, I don't think we could have remained friends." He laughs, and this time when he sits back on the couch, he is closer to me. Thigh almost touching thigh close.

"I like you," he says through a laugh, not making a move to get off the couch.

"I like you too." It's more along the lines of *like him, like him* but we are just friends after all. He gives me a smile and I give him one back. That smile of his really does something to me.

"How was your night?" he asks, taking me away from his beautiful smile.

I shrug. "It was okay, me and Batman had an awesome time, like always. How was the party?"

He shrugs back at me. "It was a party, nothing special. I would have had more fun if I stayed behind with you." I swear I feel his arm that's resting on the back of the couch getting closer to me.

"I doubt that. I'm not very fun." I turn my body toward him, tucking my legs under myself.

"Any girl that watches a DC movie all by herself is very fun." Again with a smirk. God, this guy is going to be the death of me.

I purse my lips, trying to hide the smile that is trying to escape and turn back to the TV.

We watch the movie in silence for a few minutes before Mason breaks it.

"Why didn't you want to go to the party?" It's a simple question, it really is. It's just not a simple answer.

Why wouldn't a college student want to go to a party to drink with her friends?

I decide to go with somewhat of the truth.

"I don't drink," I state.

"Is there a reason for that?" There isn't judgment in his voice, just curiosity.

"I've made some bad decisions before when it came to alcohol, so it's best for me to not drink at all." That's as close to the truth as I can get.

"It must be hard being on a college campus with alcohol everywhere you look," he says with understanding in his eyes.

"Yeah but that's how life is." I give him a small smile, hoping he will drop the subject.

He does. He gives me a small smile of his own and turns back to the TV.

For the rest of the movie we sit in silence, but I'm not paying much attention.

All I can think about is what will happen if he finds out the whole reason I don't drink.

Is he going to want to be my friend then?

CHAPTER TEN

It feels as if my body is enveloped in something warm. Like it's all wrapped around me and I don't want to wake up because of fear that I might lose it.

I tighten my arms around whatever the warmth is and try my best to go back to the deep sleep I was in.

The sense of floral and freshness invades my nostrils and I'm not mad at it. It's a calming scent, one that I think I can smell every single day for the rest of my life.

Even as I hold it tight, the warmth shifts, making my eyes open slightly to see where it's going. My eyes slowly open and I'm met with a mop of dark curly hair right in my face.

What the hell? We don't have a cat.

The mop of curls moves again and then I realize just exactly what the warm thing that's wrapped around me, is.

It's Jordan.

We must have fallen asleep while watching the movie and she somehow made it on top of me. Jordan lets out a groan of her own while she cuddles deeper into my chest.

I should wake her, but I don't. I continue to lie here like the dumbfuck that I am, staring down at the beautiful girl that is currently in my arms.

She has dark, long lashes that currently frame her full cheeks. Her berry-tinted lips are full and plump and asking to be bitten into. My eyes travel to her nose and see that she has slight fullness to it that fits her face flawlessly.

This girl is perfect. Beautiful and perfect, and I can already feel my morning wood growing more and more as I continue to stare at her.

I quickly reposition myself so that my hardening cock isn't stabbing her in the stomach.

My shifting must have woken her up because I currently have big brown eyes staring at me in wonder.

"Good morning," I say to her, my voice still filled with sleep.

At my words, her beautiful eyes go wide and she scrambles off of me.

"Morning," she whispers when she is situated on the couch next to me, a slight blush covering her full cheeks.

"I would ask you how you slept but it's kind of obvious." I smirk at her, joking around. But I'm not going to lie, having my arms wrapped around her body felt good.

She leans over and shoves me playfully. "You're a jerk." The blush keeps getting deeper and I can't help but laugh a little.

"I'm just playing with you," I tell her, rubbing the sleep from my face. "Sorry. Last thing I remember is closing my eyes, I don't know how things, um, shifted."

Jordan gives me a shy smile and brushes a piece of hair out of her face. "It's okay. It's fine. Really it's completely fine."

She's rambling. It's cute. I just want to lean in and kiss her for being so flustered and all cute like this.

There has been a shift inside of me these last few

days. I doubt it has anything to do with what happened at the field house with Jesse, maybe it does, but these last few days all I wanted was to be with Jordan.

Be surrounded by her, be near her, talk to her, make her laugh. I wanted to do everything.

Last night, I wasn't lying when I told her that I would have rather stayed here with her than go to any party. Spending any time with her would have been way better than being around rowdy people.

I know I may be blurring my invincible lines when it comes to Jordan, and I should just continue to be friends, but I don't know if I can. In the time that I have known her, she has wedged herself into me somehow and I don't know if I want her to get out.

"You're cute." I find myself saying, and at my words her eyes grow wide and her blush becomes more prominent. "Want to get breakfast?"

I surprise even myself with the suggestion. I think I'm just trying to stop myself from doing something stupid, like blurring the line more and kissing her.

Jordan looks down at her clothes and then back at me with a raised eyebrow.

"I'm not really dressed to go out in public." My eyes move from her face all the way down to her toes. Her hair is a curly mess and her mint colored toes are wiggling against the carpet. She's dressed in sweats that are way too big for her and a hoodie that I'd guess was Carter's or Gabe's. Something in me wishes it was mine instead.

She looks beautiful, but I get what she's getting at.

"I can take you to your dorm if you want to change?" I form it as a question. She looks beautiful to me, and if she's comfortable then she should wear whatever she wants.

But I have a younger sister, I know how a girl's mind works.

She scrunches her nose. "I rather not walk into the sex den so early in the morning." I can't help but laugh at her statement.

I don't want to see Damon's naked ass more than I already have.

"I'll go see what clothes Lucy has here and then we can go," she says and before I can respond, she is running up the stairs. I stand there like an idiot watching her go, possibly checking her ass out in the process.

Actually there is no possibly about it, I am checking out her ass.

I smile as I follow her up the stairs and head to my room to change quickly. In the middle of pulling down my shirt over my chest, there is a knock on my door.

"Ready?" I ask, assuming that it's Jordan, but when I open it, I see it's Carter.

He's looking at me with a raised eyebrow. The way he is standing right now reminds me of whenever my sister brings a guy home. Carter is being a protective brother.

"You're up early," he says, a smirk playing on his mouth.

I nod, "Yeah, Jordan and I were going to get something to eat. You want to come?" I'm trying to play things like I'm not silently hoping that he will say no.

"Just you and Jordan?" I can see the questioning in his eyes.

I roll my eyes. "Yes, dick head, just me and Jordan. As friends."

His eyebrows raise like he is asking "really?"

"You know what, I think that I will join you. Since we are all friends and all." He says before walking back to his room and closing the door behind him.

This fucker is playing with me and taking away serious Jordan/Mason alone time.

Ten minutes later, Jordan, Carter and I are all piling into Carter's Range Rover, heading to the diner ten minutes away from the house.

Am I mad that it wasn't just Jordan and me going to breakfast? Yup.

Am I somewhat glad that Carter came with us, so no more lines are blurred? In a way, I am. Carter going to breakfast with us keeps me from doing something stupid, like possibly kissing Jordan. Like I wanted to do last night and this morning, and every single day since I met her.

When we get to the diner, the waitress leads us to a booth in the back. Jordan slides into one side and I'm surprised when Carter slides in next to me.

We place our orders and when the waitress leaves, Carter asks Jordan about her little brother.

"Dylan said that he was going to come up in a few weeks. Did he finally make the decision?"

"Of course my brother talks to you more than he talks to me." Jordan shakes her head and grabs a sugar packet to play with before speaking again. "You and I both know that Duke was the only school he had eyes on. He's coming to check things out before he signs the letter of intent."

"What sport does he play?" I ask, putting myself in the conversation.

"Basketball. He will officially be a Blue Devil come fall." She gives me a smile before she turns to Carter. "Do not corrupt him while he's here."

Her face is stern and Carter just shakes his head and gives her a sly smile.

"I would never." He places his hand on his chest feigning hurt. "It's better if he gets corrupted by me than by Den," he says in a more serious tone.

Jordan immediately looks at him and her facial expression turns from happy to one of dread and hurt and anger.

"Who's Den?" Now the look of anger is directed at me. Her eyes are filled with anger but only for a split second. Soon her eyes soften and she lets out a sigh.

"My older brother."

When she says the word, I get the same feeling I got a few weeks ago when the subject of her older brother came up. That he's a sore subject, the only thing is that now there is an added feeling to it.

One that tells me that Jordan's relationship with her older brother is a whole lot worse for wear than I thought.

The feel of breakfast changes after the mention of Jordan's older brother.

For the rest of our meal, Carter and I carry most of the conversation with Jordan chiming in every now and then. Her mood shifting back and forth from joyful to anger.

When we finish eating, I pay the check, since I was the one that invited Jordan and Carter drove. The whole drive back to the house, I can't help but feel tension between Carter and Jordan.

He must feel guilty for mentioning her brother and well, I feel guilty for asking about him. Arriving at the house, Jordan gets out as soon as the car is in park and Carter lets out a sigh before he quickly follows after her.

I watch as he catches up to her before she walks into the house and wraps his arms around her, whispering in her ear. From what I can see, he's apologizing to her and she must accept it because she nods her head and gives him a small smile.

When I finally step out of the car, Carter goes inside and Jordan stays behind standing on the porch. She turns to look at me and all I see is a broken girl.

I don't know why she's broken, but I want to know. I want to know why talking about her older brother affects her so much and how I can help her get through it.

Making my way to her I stop on the bottom step, my hands in the pockets of my jeans. My relationship with her isn't at the hugging stage that she is with Carter, even if I wish it was.

"I'm sorry, I didn't mean to pry earlier when asking about your older brother. It wasn't my place."

Jordan gives me a small smile, "You have nothing to be sorry about. We were talking about someone you don't know, you had every right to ask who that person was. It's just that my brother is a sore subject."

I nod, the question of why is on the tip of my tongue, but I hold it in and don't ask. It's not my place and if we ever get closer, Jordan will tell me on her own time.

She gives me another smile and then takes me by surprise when she leans up and places a kiss on my cheek.

"Thank you for breakfast." She gives me a smile and then walks off the porch and heads down the street.

Well damn.

I might be screwed when it comes to this girl.

Why? Because a lone kiss on the cheek is giving me a semi and wanting a whole lot more.

CHAPTER ELEVEN

I kissed him.

It was a peck on the cheek, but hey, I still kissed him. If I continued standing on the porch, I would have done a lot more than just a kiss on the cheek.

But he was looking at me as if I was fragile and I hated it, so I kissed him and then left. I needed to clear my head after the whole Carter bringing my brother up at breakfast thing.

Carter's intentions were good, I know that, but hearing my brother's name is still hard for me.

Long story short, I haven't talked to my older brother since I was seventeen. He had moved out two years earlier after he and my dad got into a fight, and that put a strain on our relationship.

Our relationship became nonexistent the summer before my senior year. I made a stupid decision and he told me that he didn't want me to be a part of his life anymore.

I found it funny, me making a stupid decision that destroyed life as I knew it, was all because of him. The whole disownment thing should have gone the other way around.

When it comes to my brother, I only know about him because of Phoebe. She is the only person from his old life that he has kept in contact with. Not only did he disown me, but my dad and our younger brother as well. He speaks to none of us and it's all my fault.

My phone starts to vibrate in my back pocket as I open the door to my dorm, and when I pull it out and see who's calling, a smile forms on my face.

Just the distraction that I was looking for.

"Hey old man," I say, greeting him.

His big belly laugh fills my ear, "Old man my ass, I'm only twenty years older than you. I'm in the best shape of my fucking life."

I can't help but laugh with him. My dad is what you would consider a DILF, at least that's what both Lucy and Alana say.

He and my mom were still in high school when she got pregnant with my older brother. By their high school graduation they were married and had a bouncing baby attached to their hips. I came three years later before either of them were twenty-one.

They were young and I think that's what hurts the most about my mom's death. She was so young, she had a whole life to live but cancer took it away from her.

"Alana tells me you will be coming home soon," I state, cutting straight to the chase. hoping he hears the smile in my face. A few more weeks and we will be home for good.

"That's what the higher-ups say. Just a few more weeks in the desert and I will be home, kiddo."

He sounds happy about it and in return that makes me happy.

"Good. I know Alana wants you home. Maybe then you can give her a kid of her own." Alana is ten years younger than my dad, and she deserves to have a child that is biologically hers. She's given up her life to help raise Dylan and me, she deserves to have a bouncing baby of her own.

"Yeah, like the ones I have haven't tortured me enough already," he jokes as I toss my keys on my desk and head to my bed.

"Hey, Dylan's good. He hasn't given you any trouble." I gave and I'm still giving my father and stepmother holy hell. I will be forever paying my debt to them.

"Yet. The kid is heading to college in a few months, I imagine he's waiting until he is out and away from parental supervision," he grunts out. If I know my brother, he won't. Especially if he is looking at me for guidance.

"Anyway, how is my Dani girl doing?" my dad asks, taking my mind off my brother and his possible decisions.

Dani.

My full name is Jordan Daniella Garza.

To some people I'm Dani.

Ever since I was born, my parents never used my first name. From day one, my mom called me Dani, because I reminded her so much of my father, Daniel.

My parents and my brothers are the only people in my life that call me Dani. Alana doesn't even call me that, and I think it's because she wants me to have that piece of my mom with me at all times, so she sticks to calling me Jordan. As do everyone else in my life.

"Fine. Classes are getting a little harder but that's normal, I'll still be able to finish the year with top grades." I will never be at the top of my class but hey, it's something.

"That's my girl." I can hear a smile in his voice. He goes silent for a few minutes before he clears his throat and speaks, "I'm proud of you, Dani. You could have gone a completely different path after that summer, but you bettered your life and now you are succeeding. I can't tell you just how proud I am of you, baby girl. I know your mom would be proud too."

I wasn't expecting this phone call to take this turn, for my dad to say words that are making me a blubbering mess.

"Dad," I say through the tears forming in my throat.

"I mean it, honey. I'm proud of you. So much." I can hear tears of his own in his voice. A part of me knows that we wouldn't have been able to have this conversion four years ago.

There was nothing to be proud of four years ago.

There was a point in my life where my father hated me. He never voiced it and always told me that he loved me with everything he had, but I saw it in his eyes. I saw it when he addressed me, when he looked at me, when he talked about me. At times, I think I still see it. That hatred is not something that will go away with a few apologies, it takes time to finally dissipate.

"Thank you, Dad." I say, not knowing what else to say to this.

"Of course, baby girl." He sniffles a little and then comes back more cheerful. "Anyway, why are you up so early? I for sure thought that I would be waking you up."

Well if I didn't fall asleep on a certain baseball player, he would have.

I clear my throat. "I went to breakfast with Carter and M" I'm about to say Mason's name but then I think about how my dad might remember him. Actually he would remember him and that is not a conversation I want to have right now, so I think against it. "And his new roommate. I just got back to my dorm."

"New roommate, huh? Is he cute?"

Oh, what the hell this?

"What?" My dad has never talked guys with me. He usually threatens to kill anyone that isn't Gabe, Carter and Damon.

"What? Can you fault a dad for being curious about his daughter's love life?"

I cringe, not really wanting to have this conversation.

"Yes, yes I can." I tell him and he just laughs at my statement.

He stops laughing, "Well?"

Great, he wants an actual response.

I let out a sigh and cringe a little. "Yes, he's cute." I'm never going to let him live this down.

"And?"

Oh my god. "And nothing. He's cute and we are friends and that's all that we will ever be."

"I don't think I believe you," he singsongs and I swear he is starting to sound like Lucy and not the army man he is.

I'm about to tell him to go eat rocks when I hear someone in the background. "Garza, time to go." a male voice tells him.

I let out a sigh, "I guess you have to go."

"Yeah, sweetheart. I'll call you when I can, okay?" I hear worry in his voice.

"Yes, sir."

"I love you."

"I love you too. Be safe." I give him the same goodbye I always give him.

"Always." And with that the line goes dead and I'm

back in my dorm and my dad is back in Afghanistan.

Soon.

Soon he will be home and safe. Just a few more weeks.

After hanging up with my dad, I decide to take a shower. I didn't get a chance to do that earlier and for some reason I feel all sweaty and gross.

Honestly can't believe that I went to breakfast with Mason feeling like this. He probably thinks I smell or something.

I take off Lucy's clothes and put them in the hamper before climbing into the hot stream of water. There is a kink in my neck, and I bet it is from falling on the hardness that is Mason's chest.

Do I remember how we got into that position? No, not really. All I remember is that we were watching the movie, his arm was on the back of the couch, and my eyes were closing. I do vaguely remember my head bobbing and then a hand on my head pushing toward his chest and then an arm wrapping around me after that.

But do I have any idea how I fell asleep on top of him, cuddled up into his hard chest? No. Do I have regrets about it? Fuck, no.

I should though, I should feel guilty for it, because we are just friends and given who I am, I don't see us going further. Something like this could make him think that I'm leading him on and I don't want to do that.

Marveling at how the hot water feels on my body, I let my mind wander. Wander to a place where things are different, where Mason and I could be more than friends. A place where I don't have to hide who I am and my past mistakes from him. A place where he accepts me and we can be happy.

Closing my eyes, I picture his hands instead of

mine moving all over my body. I think about how his big, calloused hands would feel along my skin. Along my throat, my breasts, my stomach, my core.

Would his fingers be rough? Or would he try to be as soft as possible when touching me?

I grab my body wash and rub it all over myself, fantasizing his hands lathering me up instead of mine.

This isn't something I should be doing but the man is in my brain, I can't help it.

Washing off the body wash, my hands keep traveling down to my core. I run my fingers through my curls and into my folds.

There is wetness there that isn't from the hot water surrounding me. I bring the wetness to my clit and draw circles with my fingertips.

I picture Mason in front of me, his hand on my pussy instead of mine, whispering dirty things into my ear.

My arousal keeps growing and growing as my fantasy gets dirtier. My legs start to get wobbly. I lean my back against the shower wall and slide down until my ass is on the shower floor, water falling all over me.

My legs fall open and when they do, I rub my clit a little more, before I move my fingers through my folds and insert two into myself.

At first, I move my hand slowly, but after a few seconds I need more. I need more pressure, I need to come. My fingers move faster and harder, curling into me, making me slicker and wetter.

Finger fucking myself has been something that has brought me pleasure in the last couple of years, but never has it felt like this. Like there is a desperate need to reach my orgasm or I might faint from all the panting if I don't.

I continue to move my fingers in and out of myself and move my other hand to rub against my clit. I hear Mason's voice in my ear, saying my name, asking if I'm enjoying myself.

"Oh, fuck." The pressure keeps growing and growing, my legs shaking from the impending explosion. I curl my fingers one more time and that's what it takes for me to finally let go.

A groan fills the shower stall, echoing against the walls, filling my ears.

"Fuck." I close my eyes, trying to control my breathing and the leg shakes. Never have I made myself orgasm so hard. Of course, it had to come when I fantasized about Mason.

Once my legs are done shaking, I stand up and wash myself again, washing away my release.

Washing away the fantasy.

I can't believe I just did that. I just masturbated at the thoughts of a guy that is only supposed to be a friend. Also, who in their right mind plays with themselves mere minutes after talking to their father? I'm sure I will be going to hell for that alone.

Taking my sweet time finishing my shower, I finally get out, wrap a towel around my body and walk out of the bathroom. Instead of changing right away, I sit on the corner of my bed.

I don't know how long I sit here but the only thing circling my mind is that I can't be friends with Mason Hawke.

Especially not when my feelings for him grow more and more every single day.

Agreeing to breakfast and that kiss on the cheek was proof of that.

CHAPTER TWELVE

My opinion on night classes might be changing slightly, and it has everything to do with the dark haired beauty sitting next to me and nothing to do with the actual class.

I haven't seen her since we went to breakfast with Carter, which was Saturday, and its currently Monday. It may not be a lot of time for some people, but to me it has seemed like forever.

The urge to see her has grown each day, and I have even thought of texting her but then I realized I didn't have her number. I wanted to see her so bad, that I was actually looking forward to class tonight.

Jordan's hair is up in a ponytail, with a few pieces falling out framing her face. Her neck is on display and I just want to lean in and give her a little bite, marking her as mine.

She's not yours.

Fuck you mind, I know that. Let me fantasize.

I watch her as she pays attention to the professor and takes notes. She must feel my gaze on her because she looks over at me and gives me a smile that reaches her eyes. What

I wouldn't do to lean over and press my lips to hers. As if my body has a mind of its own, I start to lean in. The only reason I stop is because I see her eyebrow raise.

Fuck. Get it together, Hawke.

I lean back and try to put my attention to the front of the class instead of on Jordan. Taking my pen in one hand, I unconsciously throw my other arm around the back of her chair. I'm not touching her but it's close enough.

Jordan lets out a snort, but goes back to taking notes.

I'm such a dumbass.

For the rest of class, my arm stays around the back of her chair and I try not to look at her, which I don't really succeed with doing. Whenever she is in the same room as me, all my attention goes to her.

It's a curse really.

Jordan starts packing up her things when the professor excuses us and I do the same. When we are all ready to go, I grab her bag from her, a little surprised she lets me take it without a fight, and we start walking out of the auditorium-style room.

I'm about to suggest we get food before we go to our respective places, when I hear someone call out my name.

"Mason." I turn and see that it's Ricky, one of the guys from the baseball team waving at me. Looks like the guy wants to talk.

I stop walking to face him and so does Jordan. I didn't know he was in this class. I guess I've been concentrating on Jordan too much to notice.

"How are you, man?" he gives both Jordan and I a head nod as a greeting.

"Good, just getting the hang of things. How are things going with you?" I don't know this guy, so I have no idea what he wants from me.

"Good, the team is good too. We are actually looking for a new team manager, that's what I wanted to talk to you about. Well, that and to…" He starts but then looks over at Jordan before looking back at me. "I wanted to apologize for that shit that Jesse said last week. It wasn't right, he's a dick and that's not something that represents us as a team."

Shouldn't this be coming from Jesse himself and not from Ricky? And why the fuck did he have to stop me in front of Jordan? She's going to want to Ricky is talking about, I know she is.

"It's all good, man." It's moot at this point.

Jesse's words might have pissed me off but as soon as Jordan decided not to go to the party, I was good

He nods, "So, now that that's out of the way. You interested in being a team manager? We lost our main one when he graduated in December and it would be a whole lot of help having a former player take the position."

Team manager.

Not something that I ever thought of doing, when I could be playing, but giving the whole arm situation it could be something to pass time.

It might actually be something to consider.

I nod. "Email me all the information. I'll look it over and contact Coach if I decide anything." This is something I need to think about and not just jump into it.

Ricky nods, "Will do. I'll get your info from D. Thanks man, and again sorry."

Ricky gives us another head nod, and heads out of the classroom.

"What did Jesse say?" Jordan asks as we walk out of the classroom together. It doesn't surprise me that she knows who Jesse is, given how close she is to Damon.

I sigh, coming up with a lie. "Just some stupid shit about my arm. I went to the field house with Damon and he just started opening his mouth."

She gives me a look like she doesn't believe me, but she doesn't call me out, just keeps on walking. I follow her like the sad little puppy that I am.

I find it funny that I stand at six feet five inches and this girl that is nearly a foot shorter than me, has me following her every step.

Some would call that pussy whipped.

Well pussy anything around Jordan would be someone that I would forward to.

God, I need to get a handle on my shit.

Jordan stops walking at the edge of the parking lot, the usual spot where we go in separate directions. Her to her dorm and me to my car. But today she just turns to me, wonder filling her eyes.

"Do you want to come to the dorm? We can get take out or something and go over that partner project."

During class the professor assigned the semester partner project and let us choose our partners. Naturally, I just looked at Jordan and she nodded and bam we were partners. I wouldn't have it any other way.

Now the question looms, alone time with Jordan or go back to a house full of guys? The answer is obvious.

"What kind of takeout do you want?"

* * *

"You're joking?"

"Deadass. The Colonel is a scary man. Carter almost

peed his pants when he walked through the door. I don't even think the girl talked to him after that." Jordan smiles at the memory.

She is currently telling me a story from when she and my roommates had a party in high school and Carter's dad walked in while Carter had a girl giving him a lap dance.

Some funny shit. Wish I could have seen it myself.

The story that she is telling me isn't what is making me smile lie doofus.

It's the way she looks right now.

I like seeing her like this. She looks relaxed and happy and like she doesn't have a worry in the world.

After we came to her dorm, we ordered some hamburgers and instead of talking about our project we just started talking about stupid stuff. We've spent the whole last hour laughing and joking around. Currently we are both sitting on her bed, with the food containers on the floor.

"Are you thinking about taking that team manager position?" She asks, as she leans over the edge of the bed and grabs the container of fries. I try my hardest not to look at her ass and answer her question.

I sigh. "Yeah, I know it would help the team if I took it but I don't know if I'm there yet. Baseball was just taken from me a few months ago, I don't know if I'm ready to be on the field in a different capacity."

My mind isn't ready to be anything other than a pitcher.

"If it's any consolation, I think you would be a good fit. You know, since you were a good player and all."

"How would you know? You've never seen me play." I can't help but let out a laugh.

"Not in person," she shrug and then I think she

realizes what she just said because her face gets red and her eyes wide.

"Have you looked me up, Garza?" I give her a smirk.

"I didn't say that." She quickly lets out, her eyes growing wider as if I just found out one of her secrets.

Oh, she has definitely looked me up.

"No, but your face did." I give her a full-on grin now. "Just admit it, you looked me up."

She looks at me like she is determined to stand her ground. After a minute of a long stare down, she finally lets out a sigh.

"Fine. I looked you up. I found a bunch of YouTube videos and Instagram posts about you, okay? Happy?" I can't help but laugh at her.

"And was that I was a good player the only thing you learned from your research?" Before my injury, I was a shoo-in for the MLB draft, I had scouts and ESPN reporters want to know everything about me. With the scouts and the reporters came the groupies. My whole life could be found on the internet.

"That and that you're quite the manwhore," she says, unbothered. Do I want her to be jealous? Yes, I think, I do.

"Manwhore? I'm no manwhore." I smile at her. Sure, I've been with my share of women, but they always know what they are getting and it's nothing close to a relationship. Going into my third year I decided to put women on the back burner.

I would change that for Jordan

"According to Instagram, you are. Or I should say you were. You've calmed down in the last couple months. Maybe your dick fell off, that can explain why things got cold."

Is this girl for real?

"Oh you've done it now," I say before I reach over to her and grab her by the waist and start tickling her sides.

Her laugh fills my ears and the room and I tickle her even more just so that I can embed that sound into my brain.

Somehow we get repositioned and Jordan ends up on her back and I end up on top of her, our faces mere inches from each other.

She is laughing, happiness coating her eyes.

"Does this seem like my dick fell off?" I thrust my hips into her body. It takes me a second to realize what I just did, what position we are in, what she can feel poking into her stomach.

Jordan's laugh dies down and we are only left with our panting. She stares up at me and I look down at her wondering why she hasn't pushed me off of her just yet.

I shouldn't have to wait for her to push me off of her, I should be doing it because I'm on top of her without fucking consent.

I start moving off her when I feel one of her hands moving up my side, keeping me there. until it makes its way to my neck. Turning back to her, I see her eyes are still wide, but now they are filled with something that looks like lust. My gaze travels down to her lips which are parted in the most delectable way.

Her hands move to the back of my head, her fingers threading into my hair. Her touch feeling amazing

Next thing I know, Jordan is pulling me closer to her and then her lips meet mine. Kissing me.

It takes me by surprise at first, but after a few seconds I start kissing her back. Her lips are plump and sweet tasting. Jordan must have been wearing lip balm or something because her lips taste like cherries. I think it has now become my new favorite taste.

The kiss is nice and slow, as if we are just tentatively figuring out what to do. My tongue, having a mind of his own, sticks out and runs along her lower lip, asking for entry.

Jordan's mouth opens up and the second my tongue meets hers, I let out a groan. The kiss is no longer tentative, it's full-on animalistic and I cannot get enough of it.

With my mouth staying on hers, one of my hands moves down her body, and what a glorious body she has. Even with clothes covering her, I know that she has curves in all the right places and has a softness to her that I wouldn't mind getting lost in for days.

I move my hand up and down her side, until I get brave enough and place a hand on her chest.

Fuck. This girl has an amazing handful and all I want to do is take one of them in my mouth and devour it.

Jordan lets out a sweet little moan when I grope her tit and tweak her nipple through her shirt.

I pull back slightly and I see her eyes are filled with lust even more than before, and silently asking me for more.

Or maybe it's my mind telling me that she is.

Keeping my eyes on her, I ask her the silent question and she gives me a head nod. With that, I lean down and place my lips on her neck, giving her open mouth kisses, making my way down to her chest.

My hand moves down her stomach and pushes her shirt up until I reach the edge of her bra.

"Is this okay?" I ask against the skin of her neck, caressing her skin with my thumb. I pull back slight to look into her eyes, eyes that will probably haunt me forever.

With her eyes on mine, Jordan reaches for her shirt and pulls it off, leaving her only in a black lace bra.

"Fuck," I groan. She's a sight. Full tits, tan skin and fuckin' mouthwatering.

No longer able to help myself, I lean forward and place my mouth on her. My mount wrapping around her tight, light brown bud.

Jordan arches her back, giving more of herself. As my mouth devours her tits, my hand moves down her body again, this time stopping at the waistband of her jeans.

I run my finger along her skin, just itching to flip the button and let my hand travel down her panties.

"Mason." Jordan pants out and never has my name sounded so fucking hot.

"What do you want Jordan?" I ask before I take her nipple in my mouth, through her bra. She lets out another breathy moan, filling the room, my cock growing harder, knowing it's me doing this to her.

"Touch me," she breathes out and I take the invitation, and flick her jeans open, and let my hand travel to her core.

Her panties are silky smooth and when I travel down farther, I find that she is soaking wet, seeping through the flimsy fabric.

"Mm you're wet already." I say against the lace.

I move the fabric that is covering her pussy to the side and start working her.

It's a challenge with her still in her jeans but, if they get taken off, I have a feeling that this will go further than what we are ready for. That's why her bra is still on, I need willpower to control myself.

Jordan might be thinking the same thing because she

shifts slightly to pull her jeans off but not all the way. Just enough to give me enough access to finger fuck her pussy.

Finally pulling away from her tits, I roam my eyes down her body and see my fingers moving up and down her folds. My mouth watering at the sight.

I run my fingers through her soft curls and then rub methodical little circles against her clit.

"More, Mason," she pants out again. God, I need to hear her say my name like that every day of my fucking life.

"More of what, baby? What do you want me to do to this sweet pussy of yours?" I know what she wants, I know by the way her hips are grinding against me, but I need her to say the words.

She grabs me by the hair on the back of my head and brings me closer to her face. Lips almost touching mine.

"I need you to fuck my pussy with your fingers," a whisper coats my lips

"With fucking pleasure," I growl before I take her mouth in mine and do what she asked.

CHAPTER THIRTEEN

Jordan

I've fucked myself to fantasies of Mason Hawke more times than I can count since he came back into my life. Those fantasies have never felt like this, like the real thing and after this, they never will.

Mason's hands are rough, just like I thought they would be, but also there is a softness to them that makes me pant even more against his mouth.

I slide my tongue against his as his rough fingers circle my clit.

This might be a bad idea, but I don't want him to stop. I need him to make me come and we can think about the consequence of this later.

Mason bites on my bottom lip, causing a whimper to leave my mouth.

"You're so fucking wet for me, baby. My fingers slide effortlessly along your hot folds, I wonder if it will be the same when I fuck this cunt of yours with my cock."

Fuck. Why does he have to say things like that and make me even more hot and bothered than what I already am?

"You should find out," I whisper against his lips,

challenging him to do just that.

Mason lets out a low chuckle, and I feel his fingers sliding from my clit to my entrance. He slides a finger in and when he pulls it out he slides in two.

"So wet, so hot, and so fucking tight. My favorite combination." He fucks my mouth with his tongue, while he fucks my pussy with his magic fingers.

And I say magic because they have me panting and moaning out against his mouth, practically asking for more.

In the midst of our panting and moaning filling my dorm room, I also hear the sound of my wetness spreading as his fingers move in and out of me at an increasing pace.

My orgasm is on the brink of exploding and I know that Mason can feel it.

"Are you going to come for me Jordan? Are you going to coat my fingers with your juices so that I can suck them clean?"

His words are making me let out yet another moan and I don't know how much longer I can hold my impending orgasm in.

"Say you want me to make you come, Jordan. Tell me. Say my name," he growls as he moves his mouth down to my neck, sucking and nibbling along my skin.

"Mason," I pant, my eyes closing with the pleasure that he is giving me. "Make me come, please," I say just as he bites my pulse point hard. Marking me.

"With fucking pleasure, beautiful girl," he growls again, fucking loving it when he does that.

His fingers do a come hither motion inside of me, all the while he whispers against my skin how much he can't wait to taste me and how I will ruin him for other women.

Mason takes his fingers out of me unexpectedly,

before I let out a whimper, missing his touch, he slaps my pussy hard. The slap spreads my juices everywhere and he roughly inserts his fingers in me again.

At the sensation, I explode around his fingers, my legs shaking uncontrollably, a loud moan filling the room.

"Fuck," I pant out, trying to get at least some control of my body back.

Mason is still kissing me along my neck, and slowly rubbing my pussy, helping me come down from my high.

When my breathing is finally even, he leans back on one elbow and with his eyes on me, he brings the fingers that were just inside me to his mouth. I watch as he wraps his lips around them and sucks them clean, all while his gaze is on mine, never wavering. Never has a guy I've been with done this. I've had guys touch me in this way but never as good or as sexy as Mason.

"So fucking good. Do you want a taste?" There is a glimmer in his eyes that I have never seen before. It makes me nod, a smile forming on his lips.

Mason brings the fingers that were just in his mouth to mine and without taking my stare off of him, I wrap my lips around them. They are coated more with his saliva than with my orgasm, but I can still taste my tanginess as I suck his fingers as if it were his cock.

"Such a sexy, beautiful girl." He pops his fingers out of my mouth and repositions himself on top of me. Elbows on either side of my head, face close to mine and his lower body on top of my exposed one.

He brushes the hair that has fallen out of my ponytail before leaning down and kisses me again. The kiss is slow and the complete opposite of what it was a few minutes ago.

When he pulls back his eyes are filled with wonder

and happiness. "What are you thinking about?" He strokes the place between my eyebrows.

"How much fun I had," I tell him, because it's the truth, I want to do it again, but I can't help but also think about the repercussions that this may take on our friendship.

What does us doing this even mean?

"And what else?"

Of course he knows there is more.

"And what this will mean for our friendship?" I close my eyes, not wanting to ruin this moment between us.

Mason nods, thinking about my words. "I understand that. What do you want it to mean?"

I think about his question.

What do I want it to mean?

Do I want this to be a one-off thing? A friends with benefits situation? Jump into a relationship?

I'm not mentally prepared for the latter. I sure as hell don't want it to be a one-off thing, that would just drive me insane. Especially if I have to see him with other girls.

A friends with benefits situation might be a good idea, but I have a feeling that I won't know how to leave my feelings for this man at the door.

This hot, sexy man that is currently on top of me.

I shake my head. "I don't know." His face falls slightly at my words. "I do know that I don't want this to be a one-time thing. I had too much fun and that was just second base, what would third base be like or even sliding into home?"

Of course I had to throw a baseball analogy in there. How stupid am I?

Thankfully Mason lets out a chuckle instead of making fun of me about it.

"I don't want this to be a one-time thing either, but I don't think we should just jump into a relationship just yet." Then that leaves with just one option.

"So what? You want to go the 'friends with benefits' route and see if it blossoms into something bigger somewhere down the road?"

What if it doesn't? Will I be able to let him go if he finds someone that will give him a relationship? Someone that will make him happy and doesn't have problems flying out of their ass left and right.

"I like you Jordan, a lot. I can spend my whole day with you and not get bored. So how about we leave the door that heads for a relationship open for now, and explore whatever just happened as friends? I want to get to know you better, but I also want to get to know your body. We can do a no-sex thing and see where that might take us."

"I like you too." Might as well throw it out there so that we're on an even playing field.

He gives me a bright smile while I contemplate what he just said. This could get messy but it could work.

I have a lot of dark shit in my corner but maybe as we keep growing as friends that shit won't matter as much. Or maybe it will.

"It'll be a slippery slope," I state.

Mason nods, "It will be, but I think we can make it work."

"Are you sure you want to do this? With me?" There are thousands upon thousands of girls on this campus that most likely want to be with him. What in the world would I have to offer him besides secrets?

He brushes his hand along my face. "You are the only girl that has been on my mind since I moved here. So yes,

I want to do this. With you." The words fall from his lips before he places a chaste kiss on mine.

If I wasn't already on my back, half undressed, I would let my clothes fall off so that he can have his way with me.

"No sex?"

Mason nods, "No sex."

I might regret this decision, especially when he finds out everything about me and runs away, but for right now, I'll take it.

"Then let's do it then. Let's be friends that do more." I smile up at him, adjusting myself so that my core lines up with his jean covered cock.

He lets out a groan before he kisses me again.

A kiss that makes me want to forget everything.

The only thing is, I can't help but think that I should have told him that we met years ago and aren't strangers.

I should do that, but I don't.

Just add it to the pile of secrets that I'm hiding from him.

CHAPTER FOURTEEN

"Mom, why do we have to leave?" I watch as my parents pack up the car with all of our stuff. We've been in North Carolina for two weeks for my parents' friend's funeral.

My mom wanted to be here just in case her friend's husband or kids needed anything.

I got to see Dani, I tried to make her laugh, anything to take the sadness away, but nothing worked. She would give me a small smile sometimes but it always looked sad.

She missed her mom and every night I asked God to bring her back. I didn't like seeing my friend that sad.

"Your dad and I have to go back to work, sweetheart. And baseball practice starts in a few days."

I looked back at the house that I know Dani is in with her dad and brothers. As much as I want to go back home to start my new baseball season, I want to stay here more.

"It will be okay, bud. You will see Dani soon. I promise," my dad tells me before opening the door for my mom to get into the passenger side.

I keep my eyes on the house as my dad climbs in, opening my door I see as Dani comes to stand at her window. I give her a smile, one I hope she can see.

She does because she waves to me and I wave back.
"Bye Dani,." I whisper before climbing into the car.
Hopefully my dad is right and I will see Dani again.

* * *

I've been thinking about Dani a lot lately. Whether it be a dream or just a wayward thought, she always finds a way into my head.

It's been going on for a few weeks now and I have no idea why.

After that day when we left her family home after her mom's funeral, I never saw her again. I never went back to that house, I never even spoke to her. She was just a girl, one that was my first crush, but just a girl nonetheless.

There has to be a reason why I keep thinking about her so damn much, I want to figure out why, but I'm putting it on the back burner for now. I have more pressing matters at the moment, like the hot as hell woman that is currently leaving her mark on my neck.

Jordan and I were supposed to be starting our Human Memory project tonight but I started playing with her hair and now she's straddling me.

Grinding her jean clad pussy against my basketball shorts cover cock.

We're currently in my bedroom with the door closed, just asking to get caught.

It's been two weeks since the lovely day in Jordan's dorm room. In the two weeks since, we have been acting more like horny teenagers than "friends". We act like friends when there are other people around, not really touching or being anywhere near each other. But when it's just the two of us though, all that goes out the window.

I place my hands on her ass and rub her clothed pussy along my hardening length even more.

Jordan lets out a moan that vibrates all through my body.

Fuck.

I want her naked and riding my cock, using it like it's her own personal toy.

I move my hands up to her waist to where the waistband of her jeans meet her skin, and I slide my hands in through the opening.

Cupping her bare ass, the material holding my hands firm to her skin.

"I fucking love it when you wear tight jeans, but I'd love it even more if you wore a dress or a skirt, like all the time," I growl into her ear, earning me a giggle.

"Maybe I should order some." She sits up, giving me a smirk.

"You should. Easier access for me." I lean up and take her lower lip between my teeth. "But if you're going to wear a skirt, we will have to get you new panties." I run my finger along her crack, playing with the material of her G-string. "I don't want people to see this glorious ass, that's all for me." I kiss my way down the nape of her neck.

"That sounds oddly territorial, Hawke. Like something a boyfriend would say," she pants out. Something in me marvels at the fact that I make her breathless like this.

"When it comes to you, I'll get as territorial as I fucking want." I pull a hand out of her jeans and give one of her globes a hard slap. "This ass is going to be mine and when you are ready, I will mark it."

"Sexy." She giggles.

"I mean it Jordan." I pull back and meet her eyes, trying to make sure she knows I'm serious.

She looks down at me, her playfulness gone and she lets out an audible swallow.

"I know you are. Hopefully we can move to that step somewhere down the line." She looks down like she was about to add something else.

"I hear a 'but' at the end of that sentence," I probe.

She lets out a sigh and tries to climb off of me but I don't let her. I hold her in place and wait for her to speak.

"But what if you don't like the person I am when the time comes?"

What does that even mean?

"I like who I'm getting to know. Why wouldn't I like the person you are then?" I squint my eyes trying to figure out what she is getting at.

"Because there are things you don't know about me and when you find those things out, you may not see me in the same light you do now." She squares her shoulders like she is preparing for battle.

"I doubt that anything that I learn will change my mind about you." I rub small circles along her leg, trying to reassure her as best I can.

"Even if I tell you some of the things that I've done? Bad things?" Her voice is so small, if I wasn't this close, I wouldn't have heard her.

"And what bad things could a sweet girl like you do? Did you run over your dog or something?" I'm trying to make a joke out of this whole thing but with the look on her face, I'm thinking that I shouldn't. "Jordan?"

"Or something," she mumbles. I place a finger under

her chin, bringing her face up so that she could look at me.

"You can tell me you know. Whatever you did, it doesn't matter to me. I won't judge you." I hope that she sees the sincerity in my eyes and hears it in my voice.

She looks at me with big brown eyes and I watch as tears start forming in them. I'm about to lean in to place a kiss on her lips, to comfort her when I hear a door slamming open and someone yelling out a name.

"Dani!"

I pull back from her and listen again. I'm going crazy, right? No way I heard someone calling out the name Dani, right?

"Did you hear someone call out...?" I start to say, but I'm cut off with the same male voice calling out the name Dani.

"Dani! Where the hell are you?!" The male voice is getting closer.

Confused, I turn to Jordan and I see that she is watching me like she is waiting for me to react.

She lets out a sigh and this time when she moves to get off of me, I let her.

"Jordan, what is going on?" I'm confused about what just happened.

"Add this to the pile of shit I have to tell you," She says before she opens the door and walks out.

I adjust myself and follow her out. I need answers. Who is here and why do they keep calling out the name Dani? And why is Jordan going to look for said person?

When we get to the stair landing, halfway between the second and first floor, I see that there is a guy in the living room. He looks a lot like Jordan, just much taller, but they have the same eye color, same curly hair, same facial features. If I had to guess, he was her brother.

"Dani!" he calls out as soon as he sees Jordan, runs to her and engulfs her in a big hug, lifting her feet off the ground.

Why the fuck is this guy calling Jordan, Dani?

"I've missed you," the guy tells her, giving her a kiss on the cheek.

"I've missed you too," she tells him. I'm left there, standing on the stairs, dumbfounded.

"Jordan?" I hear myself asking. She turns to me, her lips rolling between her teeth, just waiting for me to continue. "What's your full name?"

It's a stupid question, but given the fact that I have been think of a girl that took up space in my head when I was a kid, very recently, I need to know.

Is Jordan and Dani the same girl?

Jordan sighs, her eyes going sad, "My full name is Jordan Daniella Garza. To my friends I'm Jordan, but my family calls me Dani."

"We've met before haven't we?" I ask the one question that was burning my tongue.

Jordan nods. "Yes, we have."

Fuck.

CHAPTER FIFTEEN

We've met before.

Jordan is the Dani I knew when I was ten. The one that I have been thinking about since I moved to Durham.

How the actual fuck didn't I piece this together before today? Is this why I have been thinking about her so much lately? Because my mind has been subconsciously telling me that the girl that I didn't want to leave when I was ten was standing right in front of me?

I have so many questions, questions I have to hold in until I get Jordan alone. Or should I call Dani? I don't even know anymore.

Jordan stares at me while I try to digest what she just told me. She looks worried, like I might explode or something. I'm not, I want to but I won't, especially when there is a guy standing next to her looking at us like we're both crazy.

"I'm Mason." Shaking my head, I extend my hand out to the guy. He's about my height but a little bit more lanky to my broad frame.

"Dylan. You're the new roommate. Dani has told me about you." Dylan, Jordan's younger brother. I vaguely remember her saying that her brother was going to come up to tour the school.

I nod. "Jordan mentioned you were coming up to tour the school." Jordan. I called her Jordan, not Dani. That's a step in the right direction, right?

Dylan nods. "Yeah, I already made my decision but Alana and my dad want me to make sure. So, here I am." Dylan smiles and it reminds me so much of his sister's.

"Where are you staying?" Jordan asks him. I take a second to study her, trying to see why I didn't recognize her but my mind seemed to.

She looks nothing like the ten-year-old girl that I remember. Her facial features changed and her hair is a lot curlier than it was before.

I'm sure that part of the reason that I didn't recognize her is because Dani hasn't been something that I remember all that well. She was just a girl that was in my life for a short time and then she wasn't. Sure, I had a crush on her but I didn't know what that even meant at the time.

The thing that gets me though, is why she didn't tell me that we knew each other. She obviously remembered me given how quick she was to tell me that we have met before.

Is that what she was going to tell me upstairs before her brother arrived?

I really need to get her alone so that I can get the answers that I want.

Dylan must have asked me something because he is staring at me with raised eyebrows.

"I'm sorry, what?" I shake my head, trying to get my thoughts back in order.

"I asked if it was okay if I crashed here. I would crash

in Dani's room but that might get her in trouble." Right.

I agree without thinking. "Yeah, it's cool. I'm sure that the other guys won't mind either," I say, before looking at Jordan. She gives me a small smile and mouths 'thank you' to me. I give her a court nod.

"Awesome," Dylan says before turning back to his sister. "I have to meet with one of the coaching assistants right now, but we could meet up when I'm done?" He looks so much like her from where I'm standing, it's freaking crazy.

Jordan nods, "Yeah, I'll just meet you back here and we can order a pizza or something."

"Cool. I'm out. See you guys later." Dylan gives his sister a kiss on the cheek before he heads out the door.

Jordan keeps her eyes on the door for as long as she can, even long after her brother closed it behind him. She finally turns to me after a few minutes of long silence.

She looks nervous and scared and all I want to do is go to her and wrap my arms around her and tell her that everything is going to be okay, but I don't.

"I'm guessing that you have questions." she finally says and all I can do is nod, getting one in return. "Do you think we can have this conversation upstairs?"

I nod again and wave for her to go before me. She walks straight to my room and I close the door when I walk in behind her. It feels like so much has changed in the minutes when we were last in here.

Jordan starts to pace the length of the room and I take a seat on the corner of my bed, waiting for her to start.

After a few minutes I realize that Jordan isn't going to saying anything. If she could she would just pace the room until she made a hole in the ground.

"Jordan." She stops pacing and looks at me, the same worry that was in her eyes downstairs is still there.

She is twisting and turning her fingers trying to distract herself. I let out a sigh and ask the one question that has been burning on my tongue.

"Are you the same Dani I met when I was six?"

Her lips go into her mouth and she nods.

This is why I've been thinking about her, because my brain has been telling me she was right in front of me.

"Why didn't you tell me?" I lean forward and place my forearms on my knees.

"I don't know. I recognized you that first morning, and when you didn't recognize me I just let it be. In my head, I thought if you did, you would ask me about it and I would just tell you."

Make sense and if I had put two and two together, I would have.

"I've been thinking about you." I look to the carpeted floor, instead of her. "Dreaming about you in a way, if that makes sense. It started my first night here actually. At first I didn't know who the girl in the dream was, until I started remembering more and more and I was finally able to piece it together. I hadn't thought about you in years but then I move here and you're a constant thought."

The bed shifts next to me and I can feel her closeness, the want to touch her grows with every second.

"I'm sorry that I didn't tell you. I should have done it that morning, but I guess a part of me wanted you to know that person that I am now. A completely different person than who I was at the age of ten. You not recognizing me, gave me the chance of introducing you the Jordan that I am today. "

I turn to her and her beautiful brown eyes are looking back at me.

"Is that what you started telling me earlier? About me not knowing everything about you?" Is this what she's hiding? If it is, I don't care.

"Part of it." She whispers, her eyes falling to the floor.

"There's more?" I didn't mean for it to come out so harsh, but it did. I know it did when I hear her take a shaky breath.

"There's more." I place a finger under her chin to bring her face up and when I see that there are tears in her eyes. This time I don't hesitate to wrap my arms around her and comfort her.

"Shh baby, don't cry." I try to comfort her as best as I can, but I have no fucking idea what brought on the tears.

"I'm broken," she whispers.

"You're not broken." I reassure her as best I can.

After a few minutes, Jordan calms down and takes herself out of my arms and starts to pace the room again. This time I don't try to stop her.

She wants to tell me something and I will let her tell me when she is ready.

Five minutes.

She paces the length of my room for five minutes before she stops and finally speaks.

"The last time I saw you was two weeks after my mom died. We were both ten and you were getting into your parents' car and you waved bye."

It's crazy that memory is what she brings up. It was the exact dream I had last night. My mind was really playing tricks on me.

Jordan continues, "I didn't want you to leave, because

you leaving meant that I had to be sad all the time, that I had more time to miss my mom and cry and I didn't want that. I didn't want to cry anymore, I just wanted to play and have my mom back." Her voice breaks and I try my damn hardest to stay where I am.

"After you and your parents left, I tried my hardest to go back to my normal life. My dad took it the hardest, next to my older brother, so I had to be the one to help take care of Dylan. I was ten years old, going to school and when I was home I was cleaning and trying to cook, just to help my dad out. That lasted about two years.

"Two years after my mom died, my dad was almost like his old self and met Alana, my stepmother. At the beginning I hated her and I hated her even more when my dad told us that they were getting married. They got married around my twelfth birthday. In my mind, my dad was finding a replacement for my mom and I didn't want that. So I rebelled in any way I could, anything that would take the pain away."

Jordan stops pacing and turns to me. Her cheeks covered in tears and she does nothing to wipe them away.

I hear her swallow, "It started with skipping school, then it went to fighting and then." She stops speaking and that's when I finally get up and go to her. When I reach her, she takes a few steps away from me, holding up a hand to stop me from getting any closer to her.

"Not yet, okay? Let me tell you this and then you can do whatever you want." I nod my head.

Jordan takes a deep breath. "I told you that I don't drink because I've made bad decisions before when it came to alcohol."

I nod. Did I find it odd that a twenty-one-year old

college student didn't drink? Yes. Was I going to question it? No, it's not my place.

"What I didn't tell you is that those bad decisions started when I was thirteen. When I took my first drink."

Fuck. Not what I expected her to say.

"I took my first drink when I was thirteen and I didn't stop. Alcohol became my coping mechanism, something that took the pain away and let me feel the numbness when I needed it. It started out with just a sip or two, then a sip turn turned to a drink then the whole bottle.

"Alcohol became my crutch, one that I was able to hide from my dad and Alana. Drinking before they went to work, drinking while I was alone, after they went to sleep."

I can feel her pain, it causes something in me that wants to take that away from her. To make things better for her.

"When I started high school, the drinking became more frequent. I had become a functioning alcoholic by the time I was sixteen. I have no idea how nobody noticed that I was drunk ninety percent of the time. I don't even know how I was even able to play volleyball for three years. Everything about that time boggles me."

I reach for her hand and she lets me take it. I give her a reassuring squeeze. It's the only way I can think of to let her know that I'm here for her.

"It was my junior year when I started experimenting with weed and oxy, on top of the alcohol. The other difference in my junior year besides the drugs, was that I somehow convinced Damon to do it with me. All of us would party together but it was me and D that would drink and smoke and take oxy whenever we could."

That's what Damon meant when he told me he and

Jordan were close. They would drink together. For some reason I have a feeling that this is going to take a dark turn.

"During the summer between our junior and senior year, Damon and I would spend almost every single day drinking and smoking at my house. One day, Alana and my dad had gone to visit her parents in Jacksonville and Dylan was at a basketball day camp. I had one job and that was to pick up Dylan from camp."

Jordan stops talking and looks up at me, but it's like she isn't seeing me, it's like she is seeing through me, lost in the memory.

"I was just supposed to pick him up, that was it. I felt fine, I thought I was fine. Damon was with me and it was only supposed to be a thirty-minute thing. Fifteen minutes to the camp and fifteen back. That was it."

Tears start falling down her face more rapidly. I drop her hand and place each of mine on either side of her face so that she can look up at me.

"You don't have to tell me. I don't need to know." I try so hard to convey the words but Jordan just shakes her head.

"I need to. You need to know what I did." More tears run down her beautiful face, her eyes red-rimmed from all the crying. I nod at her and with a deep breath she continues.

"I don't remember much. I remember getting into the car and picking up Dylan. Then it all goes dark. I don't remember the drive home, I just remember Damon sitting in the passenger seat and Dylan in the back. I remember the music playing and them laughing, but then it went dark and all I remember is hearing is the screams. They were screams of pain, and I don't know who it came from."

Holy. Fuck. The accident Damon told me about, the one that almost took baseball away from him. Jordan was the cause of it.

Jordan lets out a sob that burns a hole in my chest. This time I don't think twice about wrapping my arms around her and holding her as tight as I can. Her head lands against my chest and I cradle her head to me, as if I were trying to protect her.

She sobs for who knows how long, and I try to comfort her as best as I can. Finally she pulls back and continues telling me her story, still in my arms.

"The car somehow hit a tree and overturned. Dylan was halfway through the back window and Damon couldn't feel his leg. The only thing for me was a few scratches. How did I come out of there with just a few scratches? Why didn't I take the biggest hit?"

I cradle her head, not saying a word. Jordan feels guilt over this, and now I understand why she worried about Damon when he hurt his leg and why he kept the severity of it from her.

"The sirens came next," she says against my chest, "There were ambulances and cops everywhere and I couldn't wrap my head around what I had done. It wasn't until I saw the firefighters pulling Damon and Dylan that it finally hit me, but I didn't lose, not until I saw the paramedics performing CPR on Dylan that I completely shattered. In that moment I wanted to die. My brother was going to die and it was all my fault."

Her sobs get louder and her body starts to shake uncontrollably. I can't come up with the words to help her through this.

What do I say? That the things that she did weren't

bad? They were but that isn't something that she needs to be hearing right now.

"The ambulances took the two of them to the hospital and the cops took me to the police station when they did a sobriety test. My blood alcohol level was three times over the legal limit. How I was even able to stay awake was beyond me."

Jordan starts to heave and shake even more. I need to get her to control her breathing or she is going to faint.

I know she wants to finish this story but I don't give a shit about that right now. All I care about is Jordan and her well-being.

I grab her by the waist and lift her until she is cradled in my arms and I walk us over to the bed and lay her down. She looks up at me questioning my actions, but I just shake my head and climb into bed next to her.

Wrapping my arms around her and bring her body closer to mine. As the grip on her tightens, Jordan lets out a strangled sob.

It feels like she is breaking in my arms and I don't know how I'm going to repair her.

CHAPTER SIXTEEN

When my eyes open, I have no idea what time it is. All I do know is that I'm wrapped into a pair of muscular arms. How do I know? Well because I'm currently staring at Mason's chest.

I told him. Not everything, but I told him about my alcohol problem. About the accident. About how I almost killed my brother and ruined my best friend's life. I told him and yet he's here, holding me, consoling me.

Cuddling deeper into his body, I take in his scent, one that smells like soap but also man. It's a scent that I'm sure drives girls crazy, I know it drives me insane.

Mason's arms tighten around me some more, which tells me that he might have been awake this whole time.

Keeping my eyes on a spot on his shirt, I finish telling him about my past, since my emotional meltdown earlier didn't let me.

"I lived with guilt from that day, every single day since, and I will live with that for the rest of my life. Yes, Damon and Dylan are okay and living their best lives but it could have been very different. They could have died, or they could be living a whole different life than the one they're living now. It was my fault, it will always be my fault."

"You didn't mean to do it." Mason's voice warms me, but it doesn't give me the effect that I know he wanted to give.

"But I did it anyway and if it had gone a different direction, I wouldn't be laying with you right now. I would be in jail serving a sentence."

If Damon and Dylan had died that day, I would have told whatever judge that would have handled my case to put me away forever because I deserved it.

"What happened after the accident?" His voice is just a whisper and I hear him swallow loudly. "Did you get help?"

I let out a sigh, "My dad sent me to an academy out of state that specializes in teen mental health and addiction. I was there for a semester, and I came back to North Carolina to graduate High School on time."

The academy helped. It was more about dealing with the passing of my mom than the alcohol abuse. I didn't realize how much my mom dying affected me until I was in therapy two times a day for five months.

Somehow my dad was able to get a judge to sign off on my time at the academy to be my sentence. When I got out and went home, I was eighteen and on probation for the next five years. I had a sponsor and probation officer to report to.

Leaving the academy was an adjustment. I thought that once I left I wouldn't have anyone in my corner. Boy, was I wrong. Within an hour of being home, Carter, Gabe, Lucy and Damon were knocking at my front door.

To say I was surprised to see Damon was an understatement. I thought that he would hate me, but when

I started crying at first sight of him, he came to me and wrapped his arms around me and told me that everything was going to be okay.

Ever since that day, everything has been a challenge. There have been easy days but more often than not, there have been bad days. Days where I want to give in and have everything that is broken in me take over. There's days I want it to happen, but I don't let it.

"Did it help?"

How do I answer this?

"It did," I say in a low voice. It's the truth it did help but I'm still working things out.

Mason shifts on the bed until he is lying on his side, facing me, one of his hands on my hip.

"Let me be there for you," he whispers and I can feel a lump forming in my throat already.

"You're not going to run away?" I half expected him to, and he just might when I tell him the whole fucking truth. Like who gave me my first drink.

Mason shakes his head, "No, I will be there for you. As a friend, as a boyfriend, as whatever you need me to be, but just please let me be there for you."

I should tell him no, that he should walk away right now and not look back. He doesn't need a broken girl like me in his life, he deserves better. That's what I should tell him but I don't because I want to be with him, even if I don't deserve him.

"Okay." I give him a small nod. Mason leans in and places a kiss on my forehead.

A few hours later, we hear commotion coming from downstairs. That must mean that Dylan and the rest of the guys are home.

Mason and I head downstairs and when my foot hits the bottom step, all eyes are on me.

"What?" Why are they all looking at me like I'm naked or something?

"Where have you two been?" Gabe's question is in a playful tone, like he knows we were up to something upstairs.

"Working on a psychology project," I state walking to the kitchen. I'm not hiding the fact that Mason and I are more than just friends from the people that have known me practically my whole life, it's just none of their business what we do and don't do.

"Sure you were," Gabe yells back, a laugh coating his voice.

I grab a water bottle and head back to the living room and take a seat next to my brother.

"How was your meeting with the assistant coach?" My eyes trained on him.

"Awesome! If everything goes how I want it to, I should be signing my letter of intent the day after Dad comes back home. I'm going to be cutting it short but I want him to be there and then I will officially be a Blue Devil."

Dylan looks so excited about this, about the prospect of coming to Duke and fulfilling a dream. One that I almost took away from him.

"I'm proud of you Dyl." I give him a bright smile and he gives me one in return. He wraps an arm around me and pulls me in close.

"Next year, it will be you and me and you won't have any way to get rid of me." I push him off of me and he lets out a laugh in my ear.

"You're getting your own place, no way in hell am I

living with your dirty underwear and jersey chasers coming in and out." I don't want to be pervy to my little brother's extracurricular activities with girls.

"How many girls do you think I will be with?" He sends me a wink and I can't help but gag.

"Come on Jordan, give the kid a break. He needs to get his dick wet," Gabe throws out there.

"Can we not talk about my brother's dick please? I'd rather not have the visuals in my brain." I shudder at the thought of knowing anything sexual Dylan might do.

"Okay, then let's talk about what you and Hawke man here were doing upstairs." Gabe raises an eyebrow, a smirk playing on his face.

"We were working on a project," Mason repeats back the words I told him earlier.

"Sure thing, but then why do you have a hickey on your neck?" Mason's hand instantly goes to his neck, the same spot I was sucking on earlier. How did I not realize I left a mark?

Because you were telling him about your coping mechanism.

Right.

"How do you know it was me?" I throw at him. Hopefully my face doesn't go red with embarrassment and he doesn't call me out.

"Who else would it be? You two have been inseparable since he moved here," Carter throws back. I glare at him, as my best friend he should be on my side.

"He might have a girl you don't know about." I shrug. The words leave a bad taste in my mouth but they need to be said. Our friends need to be taken off our tail.

"Yeah, you. By the way you are sneaking in and out

of his room." I can feel the blush creeping up my neck. I thought I was being a freaking ninja when sneaking out.

Turning to look at Mason, I see that his eyes are already on me and they are silently asking what to do.

"We are just friends," I state. It's not a lie. We've talked about more but have not labeled ourselves anything other than friends. Not even after the conversation we had up in his room earlier.

I look at Gabe and Carter and they both have their eyebrows raised, not believing me. Great. I really wish that Lucy and Damon were here, because she would for sure divert the conversation to something else.

"Can we not talk about my sister's sex life? I think that's worse than her hearing about mine." Dylan shudders next to me.

Okay, I'm done with this.

"If you assholes need me, I'm going to go to my dorm and stuff my face with leftover pizza." I look over at my brother. "I'm sure you don't need me since I'm leaving you in capable hands, but if you do, you know where I live."

Dylan nods and quickly I'm putting on my shoes and grabbing my sweater and making my way out of the house.

I needed to get out of there. I already confessed one of my darkest secrets to one person. If I had stayed I would have confessed my feelings for Mason Hawke.

I'm not sure if I'm mentally prepared for that step.

CHAPTER SEVENTEEN

We all watch Jordan walk out the door and the second the door is closed, all eyes turn to me.

"What?" All three of them, Carter, Gabe and Dylan all their eyebrows raised.

"What is exactly is going on between you and my sister?" Dylan leans back on the couch, and if I wasn't taller than him or stockier, I would have found him intimidating.

"Nothing. We're just friends." Friends that kiss, give each other hickies and grope each other. Very much *friends*.

"Really?" Carter's eyebrow shoot up even more, almost touching his hairline.

"Yes, really. Jordan and I are just friends." I wonder if I say it enough times, they will believe it

"You see, I don't believe you." Carter leans forward from where he sits next to Dylan and places his elbows on his knees.

I let out a sigh, might as well go along with this, "And why is that?"

"Well for one you get all growly when she sleeps over and wanders into the kitchen in just a T-shirt and panties." Gabe drops in.

Jordan has slept over a number of three total times since I've moved in.

The first being the night of the party when I woke up and she was on top of me. The two other times were sometime in the two last week. One night she fell asleep with Lucy on the couch and the other it was on my bed after studying for a test. Both times she was wearing only panties and a shirt. I think the vein in my neck almost popped out when I saw that all of my roommates were going to see her like that.

I fucking hated it.

"I don't get growly." Is growly even a fucking word?

"Yes, you do. Let me ask you this, the first time you saw her in the kitchen with just her panties on, what was your first initial thought?" Gabe takes the same stance that Carter is in.

I realize what this is, it's Jordan's three brothers ganging up on me, great.

I think about his question. If I think back, I'm sure that my first initial thought was that this girl was hot, but no way in hell am I telling them that.

"Let me tell you what I thought that glorious morning, it was that this girl really needed to wear pants. I'm sure your thoughts were nowhere near that," Gabe says, challenging me.

"I don't care what she wears." I mutter.

"Oh really? You don't care that she wears only panties and a shirt around two straight guys?" Now Carter is the one challenging me.

"I didn't say that." I shake my head.

"You didn't have to, your face said it all." Dylan says with a smirk. This motherfucker is cocky.

"Look, we love Jordan," Carter waves between him and Gabe. "But we're just friends, always have been. She's like the little sister that I never wanted to have and the additional one to Gabe. She has been there for us countless times and we have been there for her. Nothing is going to change that. We see each other as friends, as family. The way you see Jordan isn't as a friend. We can see that she isn't just a friend to you, you care way more about her to just be friends with her. So, I'm going to tell you this once. Put your big girl panties on and be more than friends because truthfully your whole sneaking around thing is driving me fucking insane. I can't deal with it anymore. I'm sure that one of these days I'm going to walk in on you two dry humping on the couch and that's not a visual I want to see."

"I second that," Gabe agrees with Carter's statement.

I think about what they are saying, and Carter is right. I don't look at Jordan the same way they do. They look at her like a sibling and I look at her like the most beautiful woman I have ever seen.

Carter is also right about me caring too much about her. If I had my way, I would have Jordan in my arms every single morning and night because I want to keep her close.

I stay silent for God knows how long trying to contemplate what to do, when Dylan speaks up.

"Can I ask you a question?" He mimics the guy's stance.

I nod, "Go for it, man."

"She told you, didn't she? She probably didn't tell you everything but she told you enough, like about the accident? About the guilt she feels, about all of it?" His face looks so much like his sister's that it throws me off a little bit.

I nod again. "Yeah, she told me."

Dylan acknowledges my statement. "Then knowing what you know about her, if the opportunity came up, would you drop everything and start a relationship with her right this second?"

"Yes," I say without any hesitation. A smile spreads across Dylan's face right away.

"Then cut the just friends shit and get together. This is coming from her brother. I think my sister being with you will be good for her. The only thing that I would ask of you, if you do pursue a relationship with my sister, is to have patience with her. She will try to push you away, and you can't let her. She will tell you that you deserve better, and when she does, don't listen to her. She will tell you that she is okay when she's not. Be there for her, show up for her, take care of her, and fucking love her. That is all I ask from you, because my sister is my everything and if anything were to happen to her then I would be beside myself. I already almost lost her once, I can't go through that again."

* * *

I should have thought about this more, instead of getting in my car and driving over here. But I'm taking the leap that the guys told me to take.

After my conversation with the guys, I got in my car and drove to Jordan's dorm. I told them that I was just going to get some air but they knew where I was really going.

Pulling up to her dorm parking lot, I take a deep breath before climbing out of my car and heading into the building. Fingers crossed that Lucy isn't there, I kind of want to be alone with Jordan at the moment.

Thankfully someone is coming out of the building so

I don't have to tell Jordan I'm here just yet.

Taking the stairs two at a time, I make it to Jordan's dorm fairly quickly. I'm about to knock on the door, but I heard a voice that sounds oddly male coming from the other side.

No way she has some guy in there with her. Maybe it's Damon, because Jordan isn't the type of girl to be giving me a hickey in the morning and in bed with another that same night.

My knock on the door is more heavy than intended but I'm starting to get pissed at the idea of another guy in there with her.

Jordan must have heard the urgency in my knocking because within seconds, her dorm room door flies open. She looks at me confused and then looks behind me like she half expected someone to be here with me.

"What are you doing here?" Confusion fills her voice. Usually I would have texted her if I was coming over.

"I was wondering if you wanted to talk." I rock back on my heels hoping she doesn't notice how uncomfortable I am about the prospect of her having a guy over.

Jordan narrows her eyes but opens the door wider for me to come in. Once I step foot in her dorm, I see that she is the only one here. I even look into the bathroom quickly and it's empty.

What I do notice though is that her laptop on her desk is open and on the screen is a man's face. A man that looks old enough to be her father.

The man on the screen is leaned back in a chair and arms crossed across his chest. He is wearing military greens and has his eyes narrowed at me.

Fuck. If this is her dad, he is way more intimidating

than Dylan. He's scary as fuck.

I heat Jordan close the door behind me and comes to stand next to me letting out a long sigh, "Dad, this is Mason. Mason this is my dad," she introduces us.

"Nice to meet you, sir." I swallow, or should I say nice to meet you again, since we already met when I was a kid?

"Mason. What's your last name, son?" The man voice is hard in a don't fucking mess with me type of way.

"Hawke, sir," I tell him and he nods. I expected him to say something, but he just continues to nod as he leans over the keyboard and types something. I look at Jordan but she just looks as confused as I feel.

A minute later, the computer is ringing and splitting into three different screens.

Fuck.

He didn't do what I think he did, did he?

"Dad, what are you doing?" Jordan gets closer to the laptop.

"Just calling a friend." Her dad sings out before the other screen changes and my dad comes on.

Oh, what the actual fuck?

Jordan takes a surprised step back, right into my chest when my dad comes up. I steady her by wrapping an arm around her waist.

"Garza, is there a reason why you summoned me?" my dad says at the screen, probably not even noticing that I'm on his screen too.

"Because it looks like your son is doing the hanky panky with my daughter." Jordan's dad says matter-of-factly.

"Oh my god! Dad! Mason and I are just friends." Jordan practically yells at the screen.

"Uh-huh. Sure you are." What's with everyone today?

Why can't they just let two people be friends? Why do they need them to be more?

"Hello, son. Are you in bed with Miss Garza here?" My father, everyone, ever the lawyer.

"No." Is this conversation even necessary? How did we even get here anyway?

"But you want to be." It's not a question, it's a statement.

"If I say yes will this little shit show stop?" My grip on Jordan tightens slightly.

"Possibly, but if you say yes, there are a few things we need to discuss," Jordan's dad cuts in.

Fucking hell, I'm going to be a dead man.

"Okay, we gotta go. Bye!" Jordan hurries to the laptop, ends the video call and shuts the screen. She turns to me when she settles on her bed. "What just happened?"

"What I want to know if that really just happened?"

I can't help but laugh at her wide eyed expression. This morning I would have never expected to have a conversation with both my father and hers, since I had no idea they fucking knew each other.

I wonder if she hadn't told me this morning about our past history if this still would have happened? Would I be freaking out about the fact that our fathers' knew each other?

Who the hell knows?

"I think today is the day that everyone decided to gang up on us," I say to her with a chuckle.

"Tell me about it. Dylan must have texted my dad, otherwise he wouldn't have known anything." She rolls her eyes at the whole thing.

I nod, almost ignoring her statement. I have more pressing issues than our fathers.'

I take out my phone and see what time it is. It's close to midnight, the start of a new day, and maybe the start of something else.

"What are you doing here?" She takes my attention away from my phone.

"I'm putting my big girl panties on." The second the words leave my mouth, I know they sounded stupid.

"You're what?" Jordan asks through a laugh.

I look at the time again, it's eleven fifty nine. I wait for it to turn before I go to stand in front of her.

"Putting my big boy pants on and telling you that I can no longer be your friend," I say to her as I get closer to her. I watch as her face falls, and her happiness gets exchanged with sadness.

She probably thinks that it's because of everything she told me earlier today. I can see tears forming in her eyes.

"I can't be your friend anymore, because I want to be something more, something bigger and the friend thing is just getting in the way of that." I fall to my knees in front of her and take her hands in mine.

"What are you saying?" Her voice is small, in a defensive manner.

"I'm saying that what are we waiting for? We know we make great friends, but we both want more, so let's take the leap. Let's take the leap together and give in to what we both want."

I watch as she contemplates my suggestion. Her eyes dart back and forth as my thumb rubs circles along her knuckles. Jordan's skin is smooth compared to mine and I have the urgency to touch her all over.

"You really want to be with a broken woman?" she asks, her eyes still on our hands.

I place a finger under her chin and pull her face up to look at me, "You're not broken. I don't see you as broken. All I see is a beautiful woman that I want to get to know better and kiss and touch whenever I want."

Those brown eyes that I love so much, the ones that literally have me on my knees, stare back at me with so much emotion.

What I wouldn't do to have this girl be mine.

After what feels like forever, Jordan nods. She's saying yes.

She is saying yes!

"Let's take the leap." She gives me a bright smile and what better way to seal this than with a kiss.

One hot, passionate kiss.

Jordan Garza is officially my girl.

CHAPTER EIGHTEEN

There is something hard poking me in my back, and I know exactly what that is.

Mason, and his hard, and very delicious body.

I try to turn as careful as I can so that I don't wake him. He got in late last night after being away with the baseball team in Florida for an away series. He took the main team manager role about a month ago and has been traveling with the team ever since. He said that he was enjoying it and I couldn't be any more happier for him. He may not be playing but he's in an environment that he loves.

Turning, I look at the man that is lying next to me, and I can't help but smile at the sight.

It's been four weeks since the night he came to my dorm room and told me that he wanted to take the leap of us being together. At first when he said the words, I thought that maybe telling him about my past was a bad idea and he was going to tell me he could no longer be a part of my life.

I would have understood if that was the case. It would have hurt to have him walk away but I would have been okay with it. We were just friends. I would have gotten over that, somehow.

At least that's what I keep telling myself.

Thankfully that's not where the conversation went. When I told him that yes, that I would take the leap with him, he kissed me with so much emotion that I swear my lips were swollen for days after.

There was a whole lot of kissing that night, and whole lot of petting, but no sex. We've been officially together for almost a month and no sex. Not even oral.

How can that be you may ask? I don't know but I'm about to change that.

Looking over his shoulder to make sure that his bedroom door is locked, I start sliding myself down his body. He shifts onto his back and I'm able to get situated on his thighs without waking him.

Mason lets out a groan and I try to stay as still as possible. I have never been this bold when it comes to a guy before, but Mason brings something out in me that I want to explore.

I tug his sweats down slightly and then move to his briefs. I don't have to do a whole lot because his cock is already poking out.

Licking my lips, I lean forward and plant kisses along his bare chest. His body is defined everything, defined shoulders, defined abs, everything that would make guys and girls drool all over him.

Thankfully I'm the only one that gets to do that with his permission.

He lets out yet another sound of pleasure as I kiss my way down his chest and this time I feel him shift under me telling me that he is waking up.

"Mm, well isn't that a pretty sight," he growls out in that sexy morning voice of his.

I love his voice when he first wakes up, it's something that I look forward to every single time I sleep over. It's so raspy and it does things to me and in return it makes me want to do dirty things to him.

I continue my kissing path until I reach the edge of his briefs. When I'm at eye level with his cock, I lean in closer planting a kiss right on the tip. Right away, one of Mason's hands land on my head urging me closer.

"We don't have to do anything, baby." That's the same thing that he has been saying for the last month. Longer if you count are friends with benefits stage.

"But I want to." Instead of a kiss, I run my tongue along his little slit, just to show him how much I want to do this.

I lick him one more time before I pull back slightly while pulling his underwear down even more. When I lean back in, I don't do it tentatively, I wrap my hand around his cock and give it a good lick from base to tip before wrapping my mouth around it.

"Fuck." I keep my eyes on Mason as he throws his head back the second my mouth makes contact.

When we started our whole friend with benefits arrangement the most that we did was use our hands. Our mouths never ventured south of our waistbands, so I'm marveling at the effect that my mouth is having on him.

I slide my mouth farther down his length, not sure if I'd be able to fit it all. Mason has girth and a good eight inches on him, I have to try my hardest to try to control my breathing.

Taking as much of him as I can, I slide my mouth up and down his length enjoying each and every grunt and moan that leaves his mouth.

"Fuck, baby. That mouth of yours is going to get me in trouble."

I hum at his words.

"Maybe that's what I want." I say against his skin, which prompts him to wrap a hand around my hair and pull on it hard.

"You want me to fuck that mouth of yours?" Who knew the little boy that I knew once upon a time would be such a dirty talker. I fucking love it.

With a pop, I take his cock out of my mouth and sit up to face him. "Maybe I do." I give him a smirk and before I can say anything else, I'm on my back with Mason hovering over me.

"You know how to play dirty, don't you?" His words are like a caress against my lips and I give him another smirk.

"I will always be dirty when it comes to you, Hawke." His lips smash against mine and I let out a moan.

Mason pulls back, licking his lips. "I can taste myself on your tongue."

I stick my tongue out for good measure, sliding it along my lower lip, "And you taste fucking amazing."

Never had I found the appeal of tasting a guy's semen. Ninety nine percent of the time, it tastes gross and it's something that you want to spit out right away. With Mason it's different. The second a drop of precum landed on my tongue I wanted more.

He stays silent at my words and I watch as his eyes shift slightly. A smile on his face appears but then it disappears as quickly.

"Do you want to try something?" He gives me a curious look, one that I should be afraid of, but for some reason I'm finding myself nodding.

"Have you ever had someone fuck your mouth before? Like full-on cock in throat mouth fuck?"

Not what I was expecting him to say.

I shake my head, "Honest truth?" I bite my lip. Mason nods, brushing my hair out of my face. "No, the opportunity hasn't come up, but I've always wanted to try."

I'm not a virgin by any means, but that doesn't mean I've done every single sexual position or sexual thing in the world. I'm twenty one for crying out loud, no college-aged person is that experienced.

"I haven't done it either." He has curiosity in his voice and it makes me shift a little under him to quench the tingling I'm feeling between my legs.

"Do you want to?" I would love to have this first experience with him.

Mason nods, but the curiosity that was there earlier disappears is now covered with worry.

"What's wrong?" I move my hand up to his face and he leans into my touch.

"I don't want to hurt you." He sounds like he's in pain as the words leave his mouth. I can feel my eyebrows bunching up in confusion.

"You won't." I caress his cheek with the tips of my fingers.

"But what if I do? I'm so much bigger than you and sometimes I don't know my own strength."

He's cute when he's all jumbled up.

Everything finally clicks. "Is that why we haven't done anything besides kiss and touch? Because you're afraid of hurting me?"

Mason is silent for a few seconds before he nods. I

give him a smile and lean in for a kiss. "I may be a broken girl, but I'm not that fragile. I can handle whatever you give me."

I'm not just talking about sex, but of course I'm not going to tell him that.

"I can still hurt you." He turns his head and places a kiss on the palm of my hand.

Moving my hand from his face to the back of his head, I bring him closer to me and passionately kiss him. Tongues dance against each other, teeth hit against teeth. I try to convey as much as I possibly can into this kiss to convince him otherwise.

"Let's try it, and if you hurt me, we won't do it ever again. We won't know until we take the leap now, right?" I give him a smirk, throwing in his words from a few weeks ago back at him.

"I like the sound of that," he says before he leans in and continues our passionate kiss. This time he doesn't prolong it. He's pulling back as quickly as he started it.

He pulls himself off of me, and readjusts himself in the process. His sweats and briefs are still in the same place they were when I pulled them down a little bit ago. Mason goes to stand at the foot of his bed and gives me a smirk.

"Come here, baby." He waves me over, waving his finger around to where he wants me to position my head.

I move so that I'm on my back, and my head is leaned back so that my chin is only inches away from his crotch.

"Are you sure about this?" Mason leans forward, an arm on either side of my shoulders, his face mere inches from mine.

I nod. "I'm sure. I want to feel you anywhere I can." If I could, I would be feeling him whenever I can.

"Mm," Mason hums and leans and kisses me again this time in Spider-man, Toby Maguire style. His tongue slides against mine and I can feel him shifting around me and then I feel a hand sliding down my body. "Did you really think that I was going to have you choke on my cock and not let you come first? What kind of gentleman would I be?"

A naughty one, but I don't say that to him, I just let him continue to explore my mouth with his tongue while his hand slides down.

He pulls a nipple through my shirt, or I should say his shirt. "Mason."

"What, baby?" The words are like a caress against my lips.

"Touch me," I let out between kisses.

"Gladly." His hand moves from my nipple to my stomach, sliding the shirt up as he goes as when he finally reaches my pussy, he strokes me through the fabric. "I love when you only wear panties and a T-shirt when we're alone, it gives me easy access."

He runs little circles against my clit before he slides my panties to the side and runs a finger through my folds.

I pull back from his kiss, trying not to unravel at the first sight of his touch.

"Do you like that? Do you like how I play with you?" He leans his head even closer, this time his mouth coming in closer contact with my chest than my face.

"Yes," I pant against his sweatpants. Feeling bold, I wrap my arms around his thighs and start tugging his pants down until I feel the bare skin of his ass.

God, I bet it would be a glorious ass when covered in baseball pants.

I feel Mason's mouth travel farther down my body and when his mouth reaches my belly button, I pull his sweats far enough down to be able to pull his cock from his briefs and give his underside a good lick.

"Fuck." he growls, but before I know it, he is pulling back. "We'll leave the mouth fucking for another day. Right now I want my mouth on that pretty pussy of yours."

I couldn't agree more.

Sitting up, I pull my shirt over my head and turn to face him, with just my panties covering me.

"Your turn," I say seductively and I get a smirk as he lowers his sweats the rest of the way down. Standing in front of me is a very naked Mason that is hard in all the right places and I want to lick every inch of him.

"Like what you see?" He sounds cocky and given the body that he has, of course he is.

I lick my lips for good measure. "I do."

Mason climbs onto the bed and grabs me by the legs pulling me to him. With his eyes on mine, he slides his hands up until they are wrapped around my panties and he pulls them off.

Grabbing me by the waist he takes me with him as he lays down, his head on the pillow, and me on his lap.

"Sit on my face."

I swear I feel a blush crawling up my neck and face at his suggestion. He hoists me up before I can say that I am going to smother him to death with my thighs. The words are on the tip of my tongue but they die down the second that his tongue meets my pussy.

'Oh my god," I grab on to the headboard to keep myself steady but he is making it hard. What with his hands on my ass and his tongue fucking my pussy.

"So fucking good." His words vibrate through me and I feel them fucking everywhere.

"Mason," I moan out. I don't know what kind of magic he is working on my body but I feel like I'm going to come and it's only been like a minute.

"That's it Jordan. Grind your pussy against my face. Take what you want." I feel him spreading my ass cheeks and him running a finger along my crack. Never would I have thought that I would be into ass play but of course when it comes to Mason Hawke, I want to explore everything single thing.

He slides his tongue into me a few more times and I cannot hold it in any longer. Without warning, I explode around his tongue, a loud groan filling the room and bouncing off the walls.

"Fuck." I try my hardest to control the shaking in my thighs and hold on tight to the headboard so that I don't; slam backward on him.

"Delicious." Mason continues to lick me as I come down from my high and once I'm settled, he grabs me by the hips and lays me down next to him.

"I would ask where you learned to use your tongue like that, but I'd rather not know the answer to that question," I pant out. His tongue is fucking magical.

Mason chuckles and leans down to trail kisses along my collarbone. I can feel his hard cock poking into my side.

Having gathered myself, I sit up just enough to be able to push Mason back to laying on his back.

He looks up at me wondering what I'm doing.

"I'm repaying the favor," I answer his silent question.

"Babe, you don't need to do that." he starts to sit up but I just push him back down.

"But I want to," I say the same words I told him earlier.

This time I actually show him and then after he recuperates from the orgasm I gave him, he slides into me and gives me the best morning that I have ever experienced.

The no sex rule getting thrown out the window, over and over again.

CHAPTER NINETEEN

I'm one lucky bastard to be able to call Jordan Garza my girlfriend.

It's been six weeks since we've officially gotten together and it's been fucking amazing, and no I'm not only talking about our sexual explorations. It's the being able to talk to someone without a care in the world, being able to get up and try a new restaurant she's been talking about. It's the cuddling on the couch and kissing her good morning whenever she sleeps over.

It's everything.

And yes the sex is fucking amazing too. The things that that girl can do with her mouth is fucking incredible, but nothing compared to what it feels like when I slide into her.

This girl will for sure be the death of me, and I'm okay with that.

Never in my life did I think that I would be this gone for a girl. Sure, I've had girlfriends and more than a few hookups but my feelings for them were always transactional. It was nothing compared to what I feel for Jordan, and if I'm being honest, it's only been a couple of weeks but I might love this girl already.

And I'm not the only one. Since the first night with the

call with our dads, my mom and my sister have been calling a lot more frequently to talk to Jordan.

As it turns out, my mother and Jordan have a close relationship, one that I had no fucking clue about. I guess they call each other every few months just to check in. Jordan even told me that she called my mom the day that I ran into her in the kitchen, telling her that I was her friends' new roommate. I guess the fact that I didn't remember Jordan had come up.

That prompted me to ask my parents some questions about their connection with my girlfriend's family. I knew they were friends, since I met Jordan when I was six and we went to her mother's funeral, but there had to be more to the puzzle.

Apparently my parents have known her parents since they were in middle school but went their separate ways when it came to college. They had kept in touch over the years and had been there for each other when needed be. My mom told me that Jordan's mom was like her sister and their closeness grew even more since the men in their lives became best friends. My mom also told me that they even went to the wedding of Mr. Garza and his new wife, something I didn't even know about.

Maybe if I had known, I would have gone and been there for Jordan when she needed someone to lean on.

When she needed someone to talk to and help her cope. Maybe I could have done something to help her not feel so broken back then.

Maybe I could have been a shoulder for her to lean out.

But what if I had been there but it didn't help anything? Would her life be any different? Would it be worse?

Would she be the same person that she is now?

Those are answers to questions that I would never get to ask.

This isn't something that I should be thinking about right now. I should be thinking about the game that we just won and the words that Coach is telling the guys right now.

I decided to take the team manager position with the baseball team. Baseball was taken from me so abruptly that I needed something to help me with that loss. Being on the field as a team manager helps me with that. In the few weeks that I've been in this position, I've grown to love it and can see myself in this type of position in the long term.

"Okay, listen up!" Coach calls out to the guys. "It's spring break next week, and thankfully for us it's a bye-week. We get to relax a little bit, but that doesn't mean we get to slack off. I'm cutting practices from Thursday to Sunday, but I expect you to be here at the beginning of the week working your asses off. We need to be ready for when we play LSU in two weeks. Got me?"

All the guys yell out 'Yes sir' and Coach dismisses them and they all start getting ready to leave. I follow the coach out of the locker room when I feel my phone vibrating in my pocket.

Expecting it to be Jordan, I answer without looking at who it is.

"Hi baby," I greet her but I'm met with a loud male laugh on the other side.

"Baby? Are we at the level now? Should I call you honey buns?" Aiden's voice comes through the other side. I pull the phone back slightly and I see that it's in fact Aiden and not my girlfriend.

"Asshole, I thought that you were someone else." I

haven't talked to Aiden since our last conversation a few weeks a few weeks ago. He has been busy settling into their new place in Oahu.

"And if I remember correctly, you said that no girl had grabbed your attention."

He's busting my balls. This motherfucker.

"Yeah, well things change." I walk out of the field house and lean against the side wall.

Oh things have things definitely changed.

"Oh really? And who is the lucky girl?" I don't know why, but I don't feel like telling him a whole lot of about Jordan, so I just keep it simple.

"A girl that's in one of my classes, she's a pretty great girl, it could be going places." It feels like a disservice to describe my relationship with Jordan like this, but I want to keep my relationship with her, just between the two of us and without any outside opinions.

"Well not the advice I gave you, but I can't wait to meet her. Maybe you could introduce us next week." It's his last words that grab my attention.

"I'm sorry, what?" Did I hear him correctly?

"I was thinking of heading to your neck of the woods for a few days. See how you're doing and now that you have a girl, meet her too. What do you say?"

I haven't seen Aiden in months. Before I moved here, I hadn't seen Aiden in about eight months. It would be good to see him.

"Fly on over, there is no practice late next week so we can hang out and then maybe, maybe I'll introduce you to my girl." I think Jordan will like Aiden.

"Maybe? Damn, must be some girl," he says with a laugh and I smile.

"Yeah, she is." And she is. If I could spend the rest of my life with Jordan I would.

I might be getting a little ahead of myself, but it's the fucking truth.

"I'll text you all the details as soon as I know them and we can go from there."

"Sure thing, man," I say and soon we are ending the call.

I'm excited to see Aiden. He's the closet thing that I have to a brother and I can't wait for him to meet Jordan.

* * *

A few hours later, Jordan and I are sitting in the kitchen, working on putting the finishing touches on our Human Memory project at the kitchen table because if we were up in my room or in her dorm, no work would be getting done.

This project consists of two parts, an essay and a presentation. The paper is due first thing when we come back from spring break and the presentation is at the beginning of the following week.

Both things are almost done, then we could chill until we have to do the presentation.

And by chill, I mean sex. Lots and lots of sex. Just thinking about all the things I could do to her body has me readjusting.

I need to touch her.

Fuck it.

I scoot my chair closer to her and place my hand on her thigh and start massaging it absentmindedly.

"We're not going to finish," she sings out when my

lips meet her neck. Already knowing where my mind is at.

"We have plenty of time." I suck on her pulse point and she lets out a yelp.

With a giggle she pushes me off her and pats my chest. "There will be more time for that later, Hawke. Don't worry your little head."

"I'll show you a little head." I grunt out and she just laughs even more. I grab her by the chin and lean in to plant a big fat kiss on her lips when the back door opens.

"Ew. Can you guys, like not do that where we all eat?" Lucy comes barreling in, Damon walking in behind her.

"Like you two aren't just as bad." Jordan gives her a smirk which Lucy just rolls her eyes.

"Yeah, well we aren't that gross." Lucy pulls out a chair and sits next to Jordan.

"I beg to differ." Her smirk grows to a full on smile.

In the weeks that I've known these girls, I've learned that the dynamic that they have is unreal. They are like sisters. They don't really fight and are there for each other whenever the other needs them to be.

Lucy places her elbows on the table and brings her hands to cradle her face, giving Jordan the biggest puppy dog eyes that she can muster.

I can't help but laugh. This girl must want something.

"What did you do?" Jordan must think the same thing because she narrows her eyes at her friend.

"I didn't do anything. Yet."

"Yet?" Jordan's eyebrows raise.

"Yes, yet." Lucy nods eagerly.

"Okay what are you about to do?" I watch as Jordan turns to Damon and raises an eyebrow at him and he just shrugs and continues to lean against the kitchen counter.

"I want to have a party. You know for mine and Gabe's birthday, and I want you to be there." Now I get why Lucy was using puppy dog eyes with Jordan.

Ever since I found out about Jordan's past history with alcohol, I've been more aware of the things that I do. When she's around I don't drink, neither do other guys. She doesn't go to parties, and when I get invited to one she tells me to go, to have fun, but I don't. I would much rather spend time with her than go to a stranger's house and have a few drinks.

She told me one day that it was okay to drink in front of her because she was okay with it, but I'm not. I'm not okay with doing something in front of her if it's going to make her feel uncomfortable. So I would rather not do it at all.

"It can be a dry party, just us six and a few friends and that's it. Nothing more. We will just hang out here and maybe watch some movies, and maybe I'll even buy nonalcoholic beer that way everyone at least gets the impression that they're drinking," Lucy rambles on and on.

Jordan reaches over and places a hand on Lucy's stopping her from going on further.

"Luce. Have the party. Have as much alcohol you want to have, I'm okay. I will still be there because it's you and Gabe."

This is a testament as to what kind of person Jordan is. She puts other's needs before hers.

This is one of the reasons she has a place in my heart.

"Are you sure?" Lucy looks scared, like she thinks that Jordan is just playing with her.

"Yes, I'm sure. I will be there celebrating your twenty-first birthday right next to you." Lucy jumps up and wraps her arms around Jordan causing her to let out a giggle.

"I love you so much." Lucy gives her a kiss on the cheek.

"I love you too."

"Okay, I have to start planning." Lucy runs out of the room and Damon follows her out. I watch them leave before I turn back to Jordan.

"What?" she asks, I guess she sees the look of apprehension on my face.

"Are you really sure that you are okay with attending a party?" It's not my place, but she is my girlfriend, I have the right to worry about her.

She nods, "I'm sure. I'll be fine. I'm in a place where I don't even think about taking a drink. I don't feel the need to. The way I see it as long as you are right next to me, I will be fine." She gives me a beautiful smile and I lean in and give her a kiss.

"I will always be by your side, whenever you need me to be. Forever if you want."

"Forever?" She tastes the word and gives me another smile. "I like the sound of forever."

"Then forever it is."

Forever it is.

CHAPTER TWENTY

Jordan

"It's crooked!" In her eyes everything is fucking crooked.

Currently, Lucy has me and Damon, working on putting the decorations for her and Gabe's party up. Who has decorations at a college party you ask? Lucy, the masochistic pink-haired Barbie, that's who.

If she were anything like her brother, she would be okay with just placing Solo cups everywhere and having a good time, but no, she insisted she wanted decorations.

It's her twenty-first birthday after all. Her words, not mine..

I blame Damon for this. He says yes to everything that she wants. I'm sure if she asked him to propose tonight, he would. But he won't, even if he already has an engagement ring up in his room. According to him he's waiting until after they graduate to pop the question.

It's cute.

Vomit worthy, but cute. D and Luce are perfect for each other.

"It's still crooked." Lucy yells from the kitchen. How she can tell if a banner that says 'Happy Birthday' is not straight from there is beyond me.

"Where are Gabe and Carter?" If me and Damon are being subjected to this, they should be too. It's Gabe's birthday after all too.

"They went to pick up the alcohol. I think Gabe went a little crazy since he is legally able to buy shit now." Damon readjusts the banner and takes a step back to see if it's on straight. He nods. Thank god.

"Where's your boy? Shouldn't he be down here helping too?"

I grab a set of balloons and hand it to him so he can place it on the corner of the banner. Yup, this girl got balloons for a college party. Someone please help her.

"He's upstairs getting ready. His friend is flying in today so he's going to pick him up and then they are going to hang out before coming over."

Mason told me that one of his childhood friends was coming into town. He sounded excited, so I told him to spend as much time with him as possible, and said that I couldn't wait to meet him. I couldn't wait to meet another piece of Mason and to learn what makes him tick.

"Is the guy sleeping here?" I shrug.

"I think Mason said he got a hotel." D nods and we go back to putting up the decorations.

By the time I finish wrapping the banister with streamers, Mason is walking down, rolling up the sleeves of his long sleeve.

"You're drooling." He leans in to give me a kiss when he hits the bottom step.

"I don't drool." I push him slightly when we pull apart.

"My chest being wet every morning, tells me otherwise." He gives me a smirk, I push him again,

"Shut up. You said you would never speak of that outside of the bedroom." I'm a drooler, okay? It's not something I can control.

"I'm just kidding, baby." He gives me another kiss. When he pulls back and gives me a tentative smile. "I'll be back before the party starts."

I nod. "Take your time, I'll be fine. Enjoy your time with your friend." I understand his worry, but I've been around alcohol enough to know when I need to control myself. As long as I don't have any triggers, I'll be fine.

"I have my phone on, so I'm just a text away." I nod and give him another kiss.

"Go, I'll see you later." I give him a smile before he gives me another kiss and heads out.

Fingers crossed that no triggers appear before he gets back to me.

* * *

Mason

My phone dings alerting me of a text message coming through. I pull it out and I see that it's Aiden telling me that his flight just arrived at Raleigh-Durham International.

Grabbing my phone, I get out of the car and head down to the arrivals terminal. Maybe by the time I get down there, he will be off the plane and ready to go.

Aiden texted me earlier in the week to tell me that he was coming in on Thursday and staying for two weeks. Something about working at a nearby base for that time.

I think I might have done a fist pump when he told

me that. I going to be able to spend time with the guy that was like a brother to me, I was pumped.

Even Jordan got excited when I told her about him. She couldn't wait to meet him. Two pieces of my life were merging.

I make it down to the terminal just in time to see Aiden walking out of the doors with a bag on his back and one in his hand.

"My man!" he calls out when he sees me, a smile taking over his face. The man is all military, buzz cut and all.

"It's good to see you, man," I tell him when we do a man hug and give him a few pats on the back.

"It's good to see you too." Aiden pulls back and looks around for a second. "I half expected to see your girl with you."

I shove him, "I can go places without her, you know? She's back at the house, she's helping her friend get the place ready for the party tonight."

"A college party, God, I'm going to feel old." He starts walking toward the parking garage.

"You're three years older." I'm sure that twenty-four isn't that much different than being twenty-one.

"Yes, but I have a whole lot more experience in my life than you ever will. Mentally I'm a lot older than what I look like on the outside."

Is it strange that I had the same thought about Jordan?

Physically she's twenty-one but mentally she's older. And I think it has to do with everything that she has been through these last ten years.

We make it to the car and head to his hotel so that he can freshen up and drop off his stuff. While I wait for Aiden to get out the shower, I send Jordan a text, just checking in.

ME: *Miss me?*

JORDAN: *I'm sorry, who are you? I have a boyfriend.*
I snort. This girl is cheeky when she wants to be.

ME: *I say ditch the boyfriend and come with me.*

Her response is instant.

JORDAN: *Tempting, what do you got to offer? I'm fairly attached with his dick. Is yours bigger? OMG! What if it's smaller? Can't have that!*

ME: *Funny. How is it going with the birthday girl?*

JORDAN: *She currently has me trapped in Damon's room helping her find something to wear. She is on dress three. I'm positive she had her grandma send her all the dresses she had back home.*

I snort. That sounds like Lucy. God, I got so lucky landing Jordan. She is in no way as high maintenance as Lucy.
ME: *Sounds fun. We are going to dinner and then we should be at the house around 8.*

JORDAN: *Don't stress, take your time.*

I want to tell her that I love her but there is no way in

hell that should be the first time I tell her. Who wants to get the first 'I love you' through a text? Instead I send her a kiss face emoji and she sends me one back.

I love her.

I really do and I want to tell her, I just don't want to scare her away. Or maybe it's too soon for me to be feeling this way? I don't know.

Aiden comes back into the room and I pocket my phone. Within minutes, we are walking out of Aiden's hotel room and getting into my car to head to a restaurant in Downtown Raleigh.

What surprises me is that Aiden seems to know his way around.

"You spent a lot of time in Raleigh?" I ask when I pull into a parking space at a pizza place.

Aiden nods. "Spent a few years in Wilmington when I was a teenager before I left for basic training. My mom is buried there actually."

That takes me by surprise. I have known Aiden for years and not once has he mentioned his mom. I knew that he didn't have a great relationship with his father, but other than that, he has never mentioned his family. I always found it odd, but I never questioned it. What is even more off, I didn't even know he spent a few years in North Carolina, I always thought that he always lived in California.

"How did she die?" I ask when we are seated in a booth. He takes the menu from the middle of the table before he answers.

"Cancer," he says after he takes a big gulp.

"Fuck. I'm sorry."

He nods, "It was a long time ago."

As we look at the menus, I can't help but think of

Jordan. How her mother also died from cancer, but she ended up going down a different path than Aiden.

Soon the subject of his mom is dropped and we start talking about how we've been since we've last seen each other.

I ask him about Sara and how life is treating them in Hawaii. Apparently, Sara is flying in in on Sunday and staying with him for a few days. It comes out that she also has family here and I keep learning something new as the conversation continues on.

How did I not know this much about the guy?

Aiden asks me about school, the manager position and of course about Jordan. I don't tell him a whole lot about her, just tell him that he will get to know her when they meet.

From the look on his face while I talk about her, I know he can tell just how much I care about her. I don't need to voice it to know that it's true.

Once the food arrives we devour it and talk a little bit more before we pay the bill and get in the car to head to the house.

Pulling up to the house, I can hear the music from inside the car. There are people already outside, drinking and having a good time. There has to be at least fifty people here. So much for just us six and a few friends. Thankfully no one parked in the driveway or we would be walking.

"You ready to feel old?" I turn to Aiden before taking off my seat belt and opening my door.

"Dude, I already feel old," he grunts, getting out of the car after me.

On my way inside the house, I get greeted by a few of the guys from the baseball team.

"I'm going to find Jordan," I yell at Aiden when I open the door, and the music grows even louder.

"Jordan?!" he yells back. Right, I never told him her name.

"My girlfriend!" I walk into the house and look around for my girl. I finally see her by the fireplace, surrounded by our friends. She looks so happy.

I start walking over to her when she looks up and gives me a bright smile that is only meant for me, but the smile quickly disappears. That's odd.

I go to her and give her a kiss on the lips before leaning into her ear. "I want you to meet someone." When I pull back her eyes are wide and staring at something over my shoulder.

Waving Aiden over, I grab Jordan's hand and bring her closer to me.

"Babe, this is Aiden. The guy that's like a brother to me. Aiden, this is Jordan. My girl."Jordan and Aiden just stare at each other, not saying a word. Okay, not how I expected this to go.

"You've got to be fucking kidding me," I hear Damon growl behind me.

What am I missing here?

CHAPTER TWENTY-ONE

There is a reason why I don't go to college parties, and it has nothing to do with the alcohol. It has to do with the fact that it brings back unwanted memories of when Den used to take me to parties in high school.

Those were the times where it felt like all I did was party and I had no control of anything that I did. I always thought that it was a good feeling to have but the further away I got from alcohol and drinking, I realized just how wrong that was.

Don't get me wrong, I have gone to a handful of parties during my time at Duke. It's just not my scene anymore. I was done with alcohol parties when I was seventeen. I know what they have the possibility to lead too, and I rather not be around that.

But when my friends want me to be at a party with them, I put all my shit to the side and be there for them. Well, sometimes.

For the record, I'm currently hating the party right now, but because it's Gabe and Lucy I am putting a smile on my face and patiently wait for Mason to show up.

"Here. Take this." Lucy places a red cup into my hand,

and I can feel my eyebrows hitting my hairline. "It's Squirt, with some Tajin, you have to drink something."

I take a drink and sure enough it's grapefruit soda. Refreshing.

"Okay, everyone hold out your drinks." Lucy announces to our little bubble. Carter, Gabe, Damon, Lucy and I are all standing in a wannabe circle and all listen to Lucy and hold up our drinks.

"Thank you to three of the most wonderful people for being in mine and my brother's life. Thank you for accepting us and for loving us and being some of the best friends and family that two people can ask for. Thank you and thank you for celebrating our birthday with us, it means the world."

I can see tears forming in Lucy's eyes and I guess Gabe sees it too, because he wraps an arm around his sister and places a kiss on her temple.

"Happy Birthday to two of my favorite people in the world," Damon says, holding out his cup.

"Happy Birthday!" Carter and I yell and we all cheer for our favorite set of twins.

The music gets turned up and Lucy and Gabe start a chugging contest that just makes me laugh. How can a girl that is under five-two, think that she could beat her brother that is over six feet at drinking?

At least she tries.

I pull out my phone to check if Mason had texted, he hasn't. He should be here by now. If he's not here in an hour, I'll text him to see where he is at.

After I don't know how long, we are still standing in a circle just the five of us and Lucy is asking Damon to beat up her brother because he gave her water. I can't help but laugh at her antics.

While we are all laughing, I get the urge to look up and when I do the smile on my face grows even more when I see who just walked through the door.

Mason.

He's here.

I give him a bright smile, but I feel the smile disappear when I see who just walked in behind him.

What the actual fuck?

What is *he* doing here?

How is he here? Why is he here? Did he come looking for me? How did he know where I would be?

Mason gets closer to me and when he is mere inches from me he places a kiss on my lips, but I'm not concentrating on the kiss I'm concentrating on the looming figure behind him.

"I want you to meet someone," he says close enough for me to be the only one that hears him.

It all happens like a catapult. One second I'm stable and the next I'm flying through the air not knowing where I'm going to land.

Mason waves him over and introduces us.

"Babe, this is Aiden. The guy that I told you is like a brother to me. Aiden, this is Jordan. My girl."

I feel like I'm going to puke.

How do I tell my boyfriend that the man he says is like a brother to him is my actual brother? The one that abandoned me when I needed him the most.

* * *

I can't stop my body from shaking. It's been shaking

since Alana picked me up from the police station. I wanted to tell her to leave me there to rot because I deserved it.

I deserve everything that was going to come my way because I did this. I put my baby brother in the hospital. I put one of my best friends in the hospital. If they die it will be all my fault. She should have just left me there and never looked back.

I'm stupid.

I'm a stupid and selfish little girl that deserves to die. The two people that are currently in the hospital, being treated by doctors deserve to live and I deserve to die.

"They're going to be okay Jordan." Alana reaches over and touches my arm, but I recoil back. I don't deserve comfort either.

"And what if they aren't? What if something happens to them? What if they die? They will die all because of me! Because I was stupid and careless and got behind the wheel of a car when I shouldn't have! You should have left me at the police station! That's where I deserve to be!"

I can't control the tears from flowing out. I'm angry, I'm angry at the situation but most importantly I'm angry with myself.

"No, you don't!" Alana's voice fills the car.

"You should hate me! Why don't you hate me?! I put Dylan in the hospital. Why aren't you angry at me? Why aren't you telling me off? Telling me that I deserve to spend years in jail to teach me a lesson?" Why doesn't she hate me like I hate myself?

"Am I angry at you? Yes! But I don't hate you. I've known you since you were eleven Jordan, and you are as much a daughter to me as if I had my own. I'm angry at myself for not seeing the signs sooner. Seeing that you

needed my help. I hate myself for not being there for you, for not helping you when you needed me to."

I don't say anything. This isn't on her, it's on me. This is my issue and I should have stopped when dad sent Aiden away. I should have stopped when my father found out that my older brother was taking me to parties and letting me drink. I should have but the pain of seeing my brother being sent away was too much. I couldn't take it. Aiden leaving was like another black hole for me, another piece of sanity breaking off. I should have stopped but the alcohol kept calling my name.

Alana pulls into the hospital parking lot and the tears turn into an uncontrollable sob.

Inside these four walls, somewhere, is my little brother and my best friend with injuries that I caused.

The accident happened five hours ago when the sun was shining, but now the sky is now covered in darkness. I sat in a holding cell for all those five hours, after a mugshot was taken and my fingerprints were inked. I wasn't allowed to go anywhere until my blood alcohol level dropped. I was going to go to jail since North Carolina has sentences of up to sixty days for underage DUIs.

Somehow someway, my dad was able to get a judge to set my bail without a hearing, which is why I was able to leave.

Alana reaches for me again and this time I don't pull back.

"Jordan, look at me." I turn my gaze from the hospital to my stepmother. "We are going to go in there but you have to rein in your emotions. If either Dylan or Damon are awake they are going to get even more scared than what they already are if they see you like this. I need

you to be a strong person right now, okay? They can't see you like this."

They can't see you like this.

I compose myself before I nod at Alana and we are getting out of the car and heading into the hospital.

If I thought I was shaking uncontrollably earlier, that is nothing compared to how I'm shaking now.

Alana walks me through the entrance and guides me to the elevator banks. I shake the whole way up to the fifth floor. Alana wraps an arm around my shoulders, trying to give me some comfort.

I let her, because who knows how much time I have left before I get thrown into jail.

The elevator doors open and right away, I see my dad pacing the length of the hallway. He looks up right away, meeting my gaze. His eyes are red rimmed and he looks like he has aged more than ten years since I saw him this yesterday before he and Alana left for their trip.

An uncontrollable sob escapes my mouth. "I'm sorry. I'm sorry. I'm so, so, sorry." The words seem like a jumbled-up mess to me but he seems to understand what I said because his face softens up a bit, before he comes and wraps his arms around me.

I bury my face in my dad's chest and keep repeating my apology to him over and over again.

"Shhh, it's okay, honey. It's okay." he says into my ear, but it's not. It's not okay.

It will never be okay.

Dad pulls back and he wipes tears away from his eyes. I have only seen my dad cry when my mom died. Seeing him like this makes me hate myself even more.

"I'm sorry," I say again.

"It's okay, as long as both of you are alive, it will be okay. I promise everything will be okay." He gives me another hug and all I can do is just nod.

"Can I see them?" Is that too much to ask? Am I even allowed to see them?

Will they even want to see me?

My dad looks over to Alana and I don't know what she silently tells him but he turns back to me and nods.

Our first stop is Damon's room. His mom is in there, sitting at his bedside. When she sees me, she immediately stands up and for a second I think that she is going to slap me but instead she gives me a tight hug. She tells me that she is so happy that I'm okay.

When she lets me go I go sit with Damon for a little bit and his mom tells me that his leg is broken in several places.

His leg.

I probably took baseball away from him.

After a few more minutes, my dad says that it's time to go, so I give up my seat next to Damon, and apologize to his mom one more time before I leave the room.

We are almost to Dylan's room when I hear a voice coming from behind me.

"She's not going in there." I know that voice. I would know that voice anywhere.

My brother is here.

Aiden is here.

I turn and sure enough Aiden is walking up the hall to us and if it were any other circumstance, I would run into my big brother's arms. But with the look that is currently on his face, that isn't an option.

"Aiden." My dad's tone is strained and tells you he's

dealt with enough bullshit for one day.

"Don't 'Aiden' me, Daniel. You lost the right of telling me what to do when you kicked me out of your house." Aiden is angry and that anger is directed at two people. Our father and I.

Our father, for kicking him out, and me for putting our little brother in the hospital. Almost costing him his life.

Around two years ago, Aiden took me to a party. My dad wasn't home and Alana had gone to visit her parents. What we didn't know is that while we were partying and getting drunk, Alana had picked up our dad from the airport.

We didn't come home until three in the morning that night. I was drunk out of my mind and Aiden was high as a kite. I had never seen my dad so angry before, never had I seen him yell like I did that night.

The two of them got in a fight that night, with Aiden packing up some clothes, yelling about not wanting to be under the same roof as Dad. He went to go stay with a friend and a few weeks later got into some trouble on base.

That was when Dad gave him the option of enlisting, going to college to clean up his act or getting cut off completely. Aiden chose to enlist in the army and getting cut off along with it.

I haven't seen my brother in almost two years and now he is standing in front of me, looking at me like I'm a piece of shit that he can't wait to get rid of.

"She wants to go see him." My dad stands in front of me, like a protective shield.

"And I said she's not. She's not going anywhere near him. Not after what she did. It's because of her stupidity

that he is in here. She could have killed him." I have never seen so much disgust on Aiden's face.

"She's not the only one to blame here, all of us are too. Alana and I didn't see the signs that she needed help and you made her into this. This is as much your fault as it is hers." I can feel my dad tense as he says the words.

"Do. Not. Put. This. On. Me. She's here because of her own choices, I have nothing to do with it."

I made my brother hate me.

"Enough. Both of you. This isn't the time or place to have this discussion. Jordan is going in to see Dylan and that is the end of it." Alana stands between my father and Aiden before she gives me a small smile and walks into Dylan's room.

My dad grabs my hand and starts walking me in the room, following Alana when another hand grabs at me.

I turn to see Aiden sneer staring right at me.

"I will never forgive you for this, Dani. You are a disgrace and from here on out, I want nothing to do with you."

***

I want nothing to do with you.

Those are the last words Aiden said to me before he walked away from me, leaving me a chaotic mess, not even turning when I yelled out his name.

That was the last time I saw him in person, the last time I spoke words to him. All I wanted was my brother and he walked away from me.

He left me a broken little girl and standing in front of him right now that's how I feel. Like the broken little girl that destroys everything in sight and will never be repaired.

His eyes are on me. He looks the same but older at the same time. His face is clean shaven and he looks like he added a whole lot of muscle to his body.

As I continue to study him, I see the same anger and the same disgust I saw in him all those years ago. He still looks at me the same. Nothing has changed. I may be a different person but my brother still looks at me like I'm a piece of trash.

"Baby." I'm vaguely aware of Mason trying to get my attention but I don't turn to him. I keep my eyes on the one person that I needed the most.

"Baby, are you okay?" Mason stands in front me, finally taking my attention away from Aiden.

"What?" I shake my head, trying my best to clear all the cloudiness.

"I asked if you were okay?" There is concern forming on his facial features. I give Aiden one last look and I turn to my boyfriend.

I nod. "Yeah, I'm fine."

As I address Mason, I can't help but wonder how Aiden could be a brother figure to Mason, but walk out on me and Dylan?

Also did he know about Mason and me? I know that he knew that I attended Duke because Phoebe told me, but what else does he know?

There is a lot happening at once, I can't take it. The mix of the music, the people, the alcohol being around and the appearance of my brother it's all messing with my head.

I need to get out of here.

"Excuse me," I say and walk around Mason and head to the stairs. Before I hit the first step, something catches my eye and I grab it before thinking about it twice.

I make my way upstairs and head straight to Mason's ensuite. Once there, I close the door behind me and turn to the sink to splash water on my face.

Once my face is all wet, I turn to look at myself in the mirror. I look like a mess, and I can feel tears on the verge of coming out.

I hate feeling like this, I hate feeling helpless and out of control.

My eyes travel to the object that had grabbed my attention and brought to the bathroom with me.

When Mason left earlier, I said to myself that I hoped that I wouldn't have any triggers while he was gone. Who knew that I would have one when he came back.

Without thinking for another second, I grab the object and open it and place the opening to my lips.

For the first time in almost five years, I take a drink.

One glorious drink.

Throwing everything I have worked for down the drain.

This one's for you older brother.

CHAPTER TWENTY-TWO

Mason

I watch as Jordan climbs the stairs and then disappears out of my sight.

What in the actual fuck just happen? I thought that she would be excited to meet Aiden, but it seems like the second she saw him, she shut down.

Turning to face my friends for some possible answers, I see that they are all staring at the man standing behind me. Their faces look angry that he's here, angry at me for inviting him, for bringing him here.

"Someone want to tell me what is going on?" I can feel anger bubbling in my chest.

"Why don't you ask the Lance Corporal? After all he's the one that arrived here uninvited," Damon spits out, his face contorting with disgust.

How do they know Aiden?

"How the fuck do you know that he's a Lance Corporal?" I don't like not being in the know of shit, and this is starting to piss me the fuck off. I need fucking answers and I need them now.

"I'm going to go find Jordan." Lucy walks around her boyfriend and brother and heads to the stairs.

"I swear to God, if you being here hurts her in any way, I will strangle you with my own two hands." Carter steps forward, looking like he's about to charge Aiden. I step in front of him and place a hand on his chest. I won't fight my roommate, especially with how close he is to Jordan, but if he pushes me over the edge, I will.

"You have no fucking idea what you're talking about Matthews. So stay in your fucking lane," Aiden spits in Carter's direction.

They know each other, but how? Am I really that stupid that I can't figure it out?

I don't know how much time has passed, but it's enough for Lucy to go upstairs and come back to us.

"Jordan says that she is coming down. She was locked in the bathroom." She sounds angry and when she turns to Aiden she looks like she is going to jump and punch him.

"Motherfucker," Damon lets out and when I turn to him, I see that he is looking at the stairs. I follow his line of sight and see Jordan coming down the stairs.

My eyes don't zero in on her body like they usually do, no this time my eyes zero in on the bottle of vodka that's in her hand.

When she reaches the bottom step, she turns and meets my gaze. It's blank with no emotion, like she has shut down completely and a different person is taking charge of her body.

I drop my hand from Carter's chest and walk through the gaggle of people to get to my girl. When I reach her, I place a hand on her hip, bringing her closer to me.

"Baby, what are you doing?" My voice is low and tentative, trying to assess the situation.

For one second her expression is blank and the next

it's as if everything is back to normal, "Nothing," She wraps an arm around my neck, bringing me closer to her face. "Just having a good time. I'm allowed to have a good time, right?"

"You don't drink." I state.

Jordan brings my face closer to hers and brushes her lips against mine. I can taste the vodka on her lips.

"You don't have to worry, okay? I know what I'm doing. I'll be okay." She gives me the smile that I love so much before placing another kiss on my lips, but it only last a few seconds before she pulls back and unwraps herself from my arms.

"Jordan," I call out when she starts walking away.

"I'm fine, Mason, go have fun with your friend that is almost like a brother to you. I promise you that I'm fine. I'll come and find you in a little bit." There is a bite to her tone that gives me an impression that she wanted to say something completely different.

Without another word, she walks away, taking pull after pull from the bottle.

"What the fuck is she doing?" Carter comes up behind me and if the music was any louder, I wouldn't be able to hear him. "Aren't you going to stop her?"

"What do you want me to do? Force the bottle out of her hand? Force her to tell me what the fuck happened that flipped a switch in her? You and I both know that Jordan doesn't work that way."

I'm fucking angry right now and the only person I can take it out on is Carter.

"As her boyfriend, you should be doing just that. I don't give a shit if this isn't how she works." he spits out before walking in the direction that Jordan went.

Carter is right. I should do that.

Forgetting about Aiden, I follow Carter and Jordan. I end up finding them in the backyard, Jordan now has a bottle of whiskey with the vodka.

Fuck this isn't going to be pretty.

"Jordan, let's just go to your dorm and watch a movie or something," Carter offers, reaching for her but Jordan just walks out of his hold and just starts dancing.

"I don't want to watch a movie. I'm fine here. Do you know how long it's been since I've had a drink?" A smile forms on her face, but there is something dark and twisted in it. "I haven't had a drink since the day of the accident." She lets out a giggle and starts spinning around.

Why does she sound like she is drunk already? Alcohol shouldn't have affected her this quickly.

"Jordan," I call out and she stops twirling and skips over to me.

"Do you want to dance with me?" She presses her body against mine and starts to sway. Her body grinding against mine. Any other time I would have been enjoying it, but not right now.

I grab her by the hips to steady her movement.

"How much have you had to drink?" My voice is stern.

She shrugs and then leans in "Can you keep a secret?" I nod and she continues, "The vodka bottle was brand new when I took the first drink."

I look at the bottle in her hand and see that it's almost halfway gone. Fuck.

"Baby, maybe you should have some water." I suggest, about to drag her inside the house.

"Why would I do that? Because I'm a disgrace if I

drink? Because if I drink you want nothing to do with me?" Her face turns serious, and she stops swaying, steady on her feet.

"I didn't say that." I reach for her again but she steps farther away from me.

"You didn't. But he did." She points behind me. Turning I see that Aiden, Gabe, Damon, and Lucy have all joined us outside.

"Who did, Jordan? Who told you that you were a disgrace?"

"Who do you think, Mason? The guy that is like a brother to you. Which is a little ironic because when I needed my brother, he wasn't there for me and yet he can act like a big brother to you. He told me that I was a disgrace for what I did and didn't want anything to do with me. Isn't that right, Den? Why don't you tell Mason here, how you threw your little sister out like trash and abandoned her when she needed you the most?"

Brother.

Den.

Aiden is Jordan's older brother? How is that possible? Aiden has a different last name?

This can't be real.

"Dani, you need to calm down." Aiden steps forward, his voice hard toward my girlfriend.

That's when everything clicks.

He called her Dani.

I never told him his name. I never mentioned the name Jordan or even Dani for that matter. Yet he knew it.

He called her Dani, just like her father and Dylan do.

He was there for me when I needed him, but when it came to his own flesh and blood, he walked away.

"Calm down. Calm down? Why do I need to calm down Aiden? It's all true. Should I also tell him that you're the one that gave me the first drink at thirteen? Or how about how you took me to a high school party a few weeks after that? Or how about that I haven't heard or seen you since I was seventeen? What exactly do you want me to calm down about?" Jordan takes a defensive stance, and if I didn't have a hold on her, I'm sure that she would jump on him somehow.

"You could have said no. You could have told me no on countless occasions, stopped whatever you were doing. So why didn't you? You being like this is not my fault."

I badly wanted to yell out that he is her brother, He should have protected her and he should have done everything in his power to not let it get this far. That's what I would have done had it been Cassy, my sister, in Jordan's position. That's what any good brother would do.

My hold on Jordan is the only thing that is stopping me from beating the shit out of Aiden.

"You're right. I could have told you no countless of times. But you're my brother, you should have been my voice of reason. You should have been the one to tell me not to do anything when I asked. You should have protected me!" Jordan's body shakes, and I can see tears forming in her eyes.

Jordan thrashes against me, "Let me go Mason. Let me go."

"No," I growl against here ear. "You're drunk and you fucking need me."

"I don't. I don't need you. I don't need anyone." She somehow gets out of my hold and storms off.

Instead of chasing her, I watch her leave. I need to

take care of something before I go after her and make sure she is okay. And that's taking care of her brother.

Without thinking, I charge Aiden, and my fist meets his face.

Once.

Twice.

Three times before someone is pulling me off.

"What the hell, Mase?!" he yells at me when I get pulled off him.

"How could you treat me like a brother and treat your own fucking blood like they don't exist?" I feel like I'm about to explode.

"You don't know the whole fucking story!" He says through his teeth, standing up at his full height.

"You're right, I don't. But I will do anything to protect my girl, so get the fuck out of here before I do something else besides punching your face."

Aiden wipes the blood from his bottom lip and with one final nod at me, he walks to the side of the house and leaves.

I untangle myself from Damon's and Carter's arms and go find my girl.

CHAPTER TWENTY-THREE

I've made a number of bad decisions in my life, this has to be one of the biggest ones.

With just one little swig, I threw all the progress I made in four years out the window. I should hate myself for this, I should call my sponsor, I should call my probation officer. I should do a whole lot of things, but I don't. Instead I sit here in the dark, switching between vodka and whiskey, knowing that I'm going to regret everything tomorrow.

But I don't care anymore.

I don't care right now.

I need to get rid of the pain of seeing my brother. I need something to feel numbness because I can't stop thinking that my brother chose to be an older brother to someone else but not to me.

How did I let this blindside me? I knew that Aiden was still in contact with Phoebe and Cole, Mason's dad and I knew that Mason knew him. How can I also be so stupid and not know that Aiden was the friend that was flying in? *Because Mason never said his name.*

I should kick him in the nuts for that.

Yet, I didn't know that Mason saw him as an older

brother? How is that possible?

How did I not know that?

I understand that Aiden and my dad don't have a relationship, and the one with me is also nonexistent, but he also destroyed his relationship with Dylan. In the four years since I last saw him, he hasn't talked to Dylan once. I know this because Dylan would have told me otherwise.

I think that's what hurts the most. That for a period of time, Dylan didn't have either me or Aiden, but I went back. Aiden didn't.

Taking that first drink after four years, felt good. It felt like I was in control again, like I was on stable ground and nobody could touch me or hurt me.

The only person that was able to hurt me was me, and I was okay with that.

I take another drink from the vodka bottle, but no more liquid comes out of it. Staring down at it, I see that it's empty. To most people drinking a whole bottle of vodka would mean puking their guts out. For me, since I had years to build my tolerance, it will take a lot more to destroy me.

Sure it hit me fast, but I can still function with this amount of alcohol in my body. How you may ask? I have no fucking idea, I should be passed out somewhere, not reaching for another bottle.

I grab the whiskey and take a drink. This one is still pretty full and should be able to last me a few hours. Vodka is my weakness and whiskey is my salvation.

I have no idea how long I sit here in the dark, but it's not long enough before a fist starts hitting against my dorm room door.

I was wondering how long it would take him to find me.

When I left the guys' house I should have gone somewhere where they wouldn't find me when they inevitably came looking for me. But stupid me, decided to just come to my dorm, hopping no one would come.

But of course someone came. Not one of my friends or Mason would let me go down a dark spiral.

"Jordan. I know you're in there. Open the door." Mason's voice rings through the room. I so badly want to just throw the door open and fall into his arms. But I can't.

I can't let him see me like this.

"Baby, please. Just open the door, so that I know that you're okay." His voice sounds like he's in pain and just hearing him like that breaks me even more.

There is another knock followed by a large thud. He must have kicked it out of frustration.

"Jordan, please open the door." I can't Mason. I just can't.

I stand up from my place on the floor and head to the door. I know he hears me shuffling around and sees my possible shadow under the door.

Standing on my tippy toes, I lean forward to look out of the peephole. I see Mason with his hands on either side of the doorframe, with his head bowed down. He looks defeated and it's all my fault.

"I'm not leaving. I'm going to stand here all fucking night if I have too. But I'm not leaving here until you open the door and let me in."

Twist the knob, Jordan. Twist the knob and let him in. Let him in because you love him and he deserves to know everything about you.

And I do. I do love him.

Tears form in my eyes just thinking about it. What

happens if I let him in and he tells me that he wants nothing to do with me?

You'll be okay. You know you will.

But will I? Will I really be okay if Mason walks out my life just like Aiden did? I know I told myself in the past that I would, that I would be okay. But that was when I was in better control of myself. When I was sober and not almost two bottles in.

Mason knows me as the Jordan that was able to conquer all the hard shit. He knows nothing of the Jordan that uses alcohol to avoid life, he just knows what I told him. He has never seen it with his own eyes. I wanted to hide that side of me from him so fucking much and everything is now crumbling around me. I no longer can hide that person from him, I will no longer be the girl that he first got together with.

Not after this.

"Please, baby." A man like Mason Hawke should never sound this broken and defeated. This is what I did to him, I made him like this.

Mason Hawke should be living his best life and not worry about the broken girl that has more issues than she could deal with. He needs to be with someone that has their shit figured out and isn't going to combust when someone walks back into their life.

But I can't tell him that unless I open the door and face him.

Taking a deep breath, I let the tears fall from my eyes and open the door.

There is the beautiful man that I love so much and some way or another I have to let him go.

That's what's best for him.

I have to let him go.

CHAPTER TWENTY-FOUR

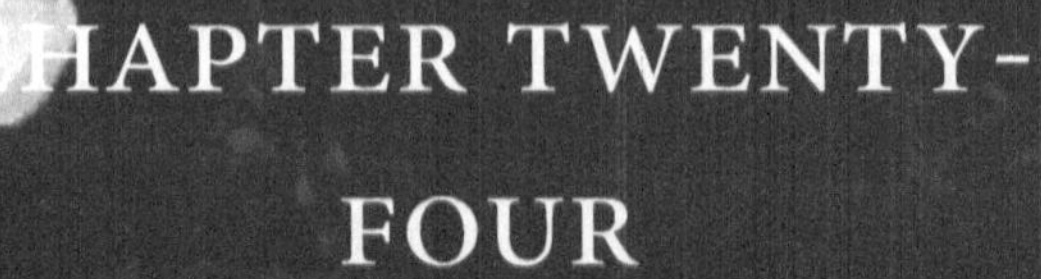

The door opens slowly and I have to restrain myself from pushing it wide open and taking her into my arms.

Her face is what I see first. Those brown eyes that I will kill to see every single day for the rest of my life, are red and have tears coming from them. Her chin is trembling and if I didn't know why there are tears rolling down her beautiful face, there would be hell to pay.

"Can I come in?" I ask her. I spent the last forty minutes looking for her. I looked through the whole house and called and texted her phone a number of times before I found her phone in the bathroom. Then when I finally decided to come to her dorm and see if she was here.

Jordan nods and opens the door wider for me to come in. I walk in and when I reach the bedroom, I see an empty bottle of vodka on the floor and the bottle of whiskey sitting right next to it.

How is she still standing?

"What are you doing here Mason?" I hear the door close and when I turn, I see that she has her arms wrapped around herself.

"I needed to make sure that you were okay." I walk closer to her but she takes a step back. Like she doesn't want me to touch her.

"I'm fine," she lets out, a little too quickly for my taste.

"No, you're not." I step closer this time, holding my hands up in surrender. Thankfully this time she doesn't step back.

Jordan looks up at me with big brown eyes filled with tears. They are red and seem like they are covered in a daze from the alcohol.

Slowly I approach her, my hands out for her to see, so that she could see what my intentions are.

I step closer and closer to her half expecting her to step back from me or to push me away from her.

Yet, she doesn't.

Jordan just stands there, watching me approach her. I watch and tears start falling out of the corner of her eyes, my hand itching to reach out and wipe them away.

She's hurting.

She's hurting so deeply, I don't know if me being here will do anything to help repair her but I have to at least try.

One final step and I'm mere inches away from her. Reaching up, I cup her cheeks, wiping the tears away. My hands travel down from her cheeks to her body until they are at her waist. I pull her closer to me and I thank the Gods looking down upon us over and over again when she doesn't pull away. She lets me take her in my arms and I hold her as tight as I possibly can without crushing her.

"I'm here for you."

Those words feel too simple for what this night has been.

Yet they are enough to brake her even more. She borrows into my chest breaking down into a sob.

I just hold her.

I will hold her until she no longer needs me to.

* * *

Hours.

That's how long it has been since Jordan left the party and I came to her dorm to look for her.

Hours since I walked in and she broke down in my arms.

A few minutes after the sobs that she were releasing filled the room, I shifted us to lie on the bed. Neither one of us slept.

Jordan just let me hold her, and that was perfectly fine with me.

But something is weighting heavy on my chest, something that I need to get out, so that she knows the truth. So that she knows that I wasn't trying to hurt her intentionally.

"I didn't know."

I've been fighting with myself over this, so many questions are rolling through my head.

One of the main ones is that how do I not remember meeting Aiden when my family and I were at their mother's funeral? How is that something I don't remember doing?

Jordan nods against my chest, "I know."

"But how didn't I know? I went to your mom's funeral. How do I not remember meeting him there? I remember you having two brothers, but I don't remember him. I spent two weeks at your house, and I met you four years before that. How can it be that I didn't meet Aiden up until a few years ago?"

Am I going crazy? Is my brain playing tricks on me,

is that what's going on?

With a sigh, Jordan sits up and looks down to face me. The tears that she cried earlier in the night almost completely dry.

Her beautiful brown eyes are red from the tears.

"When my mom died, Aiden didn't leave his room much. He went to the service and the funeral but that was it. The day after the funeral he went to stay with my grandparents in California for a little bit. He came back a few days after you left."

Okay, makes a little bit of sense. "Your last name is Garza. How is he your brother?"

Jordan scoot out of my reach and goes to sit at the foot of her bed. I sit up and scoot closer to her, my knees touching hers, taking her hands in mine.

"He's my half-brother. My mom was dating some other guy, before she met my dad, when she got pregnant. She was a junior and his dad was a senior. His biological dad didn't want anything to do with him, and left her. My dad in a way picked up all the broken pieces and they became close, so close that they fell in love. My dad was there every step of the way, and they got married a few months after Aiden was born. My dad adopted him a few months after that."

I'm about to say something but she continues. "I didn't know he had a different dad. He had the same last name as me and my dad didn't treat him any different than he treated Dylan or me. But he found out somehow, because one night we came home from a party and my dad caught us stumbling home drunk and Aiden yelled it out. They got into a big argument and my dad told Aiden what his options were if he wanted to continue living under his roof. That's when Aiden yelled out that he wasn't his real son, and that he couldn't tell him what to do. He left that night and somehow still decided to enlist in the army. He ended up changing his last name to his biological dad's to spite the man that raised him. The next time I saw him was when the accident happened. I have no idea how he found out. But he did and he went to the hospital and wanted to keep me from seeing Dylan. That's when he told me that he didn't want anything to do with me anymore."

Tears fall onto the skin on my hand, so I shift next to her and thankfully she lets me wrap my arms around her.

"Did he really give you your first drink?" Jordan nods.

I let out a long sigh.

"I was thirteen and he was drunk in his room. He told me how he used alcohol to get rid of the pain so I asked him if it could get rid of mine too. He then handed me the bottle. It became this routine until we were partying together with his high school friends. We did that until he left."

I understand drinking as a teenager, it's a somewhat normal thing. But Aiden showed Jordan some of the benefits, or in this case the drawbacks of alcohol and how it can fix or destroy things.

"He was my best friend. After he left the first time, I didn't know how to handle myself any more than when my mom died. I just kept drinking and drinking until I could no longer go a day without drinking half a bottle. All his friends knew me, so it was easy to get alcohol. It was like going to a candy store and not having a limit on what you can spend."

Hearing her words, breaks me. It's hard to comprehend just how much pain this girl has gone through in a very short life.

We stay silent for a little bit, just Jordan wrapped around in my arms and I'm sure she is thinking about what a shit show tonight turned out to be.

"I drank alcohol tonight. I finished a whole bottle," she says against my chest.

"Everything will be okay." It's a stupid thing for me to say but what else can you say in a situation like this? You will be able to work through it? You'll go back to being sober tomorrow?

That isn't how shit works.

"It won't. It won't be okay." She pulls back and looks into my eyes.

"It will be. This is just a step that you have to overcome. Give it some time then everything will be okay." I regret the words the second that they leave my mouth.

"This isn't just a step, Mason. This is something that I will have to deal with my whole life and I can't go into a pattern that when something happens to me, I pick up a bottle. That pattern can be deadly, both for me and for other people." She gets up from the bed and starts pacing the length of her room.

"We'll figure something out. Whatever you want to do, we will figure it out."

Jordan stops at my words and looks at me.

"We?" Her eyes go wide.

"Yes, we. I'm not going anywhere Jordan. I'm going to be by your side every step of the way. Whether you want me there or not." I stand up and go to her and place my hands on either side of her face.

"What about your relationship with Aiden?" Her voice is small when she asks the question.

Closing my eyes, I let out a sigh, "I don't know where

I stand with him, but you're more important."

"But he's like a brother to you."

"But he's your actual brother that cut you out of his life completely. If I had to choose between you and Aiden, I'd choose you, Dani."

The last part catches both of us by surprise. In the time that I have known that Jordan was Dani, I have always called her Jordan. It just made sense.

"You called me Dani."

I nod, "That's what your family calls you, and I want to be your family." I lean in and give her lips a kiss that I've been wanting to give her since all of this started.

I kiss her nice and slow and she melts into my body. I try to portray everything that I want to say with this one kiss.

Lifting her up, I walk her over to her bed and lay her down, her head against the pillows. I kiss her more fiercely and as the minutes go by, I feel a wetness on my lips that isn't from the kiss.

Pulling away from her, I see that the wetness is coming from the silent tears that she is shedding.

"You deserve so much better than what I have given you. You don't need someone in your life that has an alcohol problem at twenty-one, and has lived a shit life. You deserve so much more than that." Her hand caresses my cheek and I can't help but lean into her touch.

"I just want you." I place a kiss on the inside of her hand.

Jordan brings my mouth back to hers and she kisses me with as much passion as I was kissing her.

The only difference between my kiss and hers, is that hers feels like a goodbye.

CHAPTER TWENTY-FIVE

Jordan

Is it wrong not to regret what you have done? Does that make me a bad person or just someone who is human?

Because as I looked at myself in the mirror, I see someone completely different. I see someone who decided to do something that she hasn't done in four years, and I don't regret a damn thing.

Not the drinking, not finishing the whole bottle. Nothing. All that my head is thinking about is when I can get my next drink. That thought alone could be deadly.

Sometime around four in the morning, I finally fell asleep in Mason arms. We kissed for God knows how long, but didn't go further. I wasn't in the right headspace to go that far, even if I wanted to. Headspace and alcohol don't make a very good combination when it comes to sex, sorry.

I woke up about two hours after falling asleep. Before Mason was even awake, I got dressed really quickly and wrote him a note saying something about how I had to clear my head, and left my dorm.

I didn't lie, I did need to clear my head, but my drinking wasn't the only thing that I had to clear my head about. When I checked my phone after I woke up, I had a text message from a number I haven't seen pop up on my screen in years.

Aiden.

He wanted to meet.

I debated not answering him, to ignore him just like he has ignored me these last few years, but I couldn't make myself do that. I couldn't just ignore him when he wanted to meet up and talk. Even if that conversation might leave me in tears.

I said before that I thought Lucy was masochist but I might be the worse one.

I take one final look at myself in the mirror of the bathroom in a coffee house and I walk out without so much of a pep talk.

Sitting down at a table in the back, I drink my coffee and wait for my brother to arrive. I got here way earlier than the time he told me, but I wanted to get here early so that I didn't go to a liquor store and get my next fix. Since Mason poured the remainder of the whiskey down the drain.

I should have told him that when someone wants something, they will find a way to get it. No matter what.

The bell above the cafe door rings and Aiden walks in. Gotta love a military man that is punctual. He looks around until he finds where I'm sitting, then he walks over to me.

He doesn't say anything as he approaches the table or when he pulls out a chair and takes a seat. His eyes stay focused on me, and I can see his jaw tighten up.

Well, this should be fun.

"Hi." I break the tense silence and slide the second coffee cup over to him. "I got you a coffee, black. I didn't know how you took it now."

He gives me a silent 'thank you' before he picks up the cup and takes a drink. He finally speaks when the cup lands back on the table. "Black is good."

Good to know.

Aiden and I go back to staring at each other and after a few minutes he must grow tired of it because he's the one that breaks the silence next.

"How are you feeling this morning?" I guess we are going to ignore why he summoned me here.

"Nothing I can't handle." I've handled my fair share of hangovers in my short life, I can handle one more.

"Good." He nods before he lets out a sigh and places his elbows on the table, leaning closer to me. "I want to apologize."

I can't help but snort. "For what exactly? Showing up with my boyfriend and causing me to spiral down the rabbit hole?" If he hadn't shown up last night, I would have been fine. Everything would be okay right now.

Aiden shakes his head. "Yes, and no. I'm sorry that I blindsided you last night, I didn't know you and Mason were even together. It's not like he posts pictures of your face on Instagram."

He doesn't, and neither do I. If we post pictures of each other on social media, we usually keep faces out. There are certain things we want to keep for ourselves.

"But I'm also sorry for everything else. You were right last night, you're not the only one to blame for your actions, I am too. I was the one that put the first bottle in your hand, I made you think it was okay, that it was the only way to get rid of the pain and it wasn't. I'm so sorry that I didn't protect you as much as I should have. I should have been a better role model for you and Dylan and I wasn't." There is a break in his voice, and when I hear it I can't hold on to my tears any longer.

"I almost killed our brother, and my friend." I try my hardest to push down the lump in my throat but I can't. "You had a right to be angry with me."

"I could have been angry with you but still could have been there for you. Just like Dad and Alana were. Just like your friends were. I should have followed their lead but I let the anger take over me and took that anger out on you instead." There are tears forming in his eyes, and that sight just makes the lump in my throat grow even more.

The only other time that I have seen my brother cry was when our mom died.

"I understand why you did it." I hold out my hand on top of the table for him to take and it surprises me slightly when he does.

We cry silently for a few minutes, with people who are moving around the cafe occasionally looking in our direction wondering what the hell is wrong with that.

"I know it may take a while before we can forgive each other, and that we are both different people now." He takes a deep breath and then continues. "But I would really like my sister back. My family. How about we figure out a way to build that relationship back up?"

Building a relationship that we once had?

Can it be done?

What relationship would it be? The one we had before I drove into a tree? Or the one we had before our mom died?

Not giving it any more thought I nod my head. "I would like that and I'm sure that Dylan would too."

Aiden gives me a tear-stricken smile, "What about Dad?"

He called him 'dad' earlier, but I thought that it was a fluke, but now I know it wasn't.

"Is that what you want?" They both said some pretty nasty stuff to each other when they fought all those years ago. I don't know how they can repair it.

Aiden gives me a curt nod. "I do. He raised me. He made me into the man that I am today. I only cared about myself back then and I turned a blind eye to the man that saw me as a son and only that."

"He never saw you as a burden," I state.

"No, he did not. He loved me like any father would and I destroyed that because I was angry." Aiden's eyes move to the table between us, like he is contemplating something.

"I think he would like to build your relationship up again too." Because he would.

Aiden gives me a smile before he lets out a chuckle. "God, we're both a mess."

I can't help but laugh at his statement. I grab a napkin from the pile on the table and at least try to clean my face.

Good thing I didn't put on any makeup this morning.

"That we are," I respond. I give him a smile that doesn't really reach my eyes.

Where do we go from here? Do we act like siblings again? Or like the complete strangers we are?

I don't know but it's a little awkward.

The one thing I do is let go of his hand and take a drink from my coffee.

"So you and Mason? How did that happen?" Oh my god, he wants to talk to me about Mason? That's not going to be awkward at all.

"Um, I guess the crush I had on him when I was ten never went away, and when he moved here we just got to know each other." That's the simple version.

"Did he know that you were the same girl from when you were ten?"

I shake my head.

I wonder how this whole thing would have turned out if he did.

"Understandable. You look a lot different now that you're older. A lot more like Mom." I swallow, I thought the same thing.

"Yeah."

"He cares about you. A lot." It's not a question, it's a statement.

"Is that why your face is all bruised up, because he cares?" His swollen face was the first thing I saw when he walked in. I wasn't going to bring it up.

"Even with a bad arm, that boy has a mean right hook." Aiden takes a drink of his coffee.

"He's no boy, that's for sure."

Aiden spits out his coffee at my words. Oops.

"Fuck." He grabs a napkin and wipes his face clean. "I deserved that, but for now on, I'd rather not know how much not a boy he is."

"If you say so." I say, taking another drink if my coffee. When he is cleaning his face, I see the other thing that I noticed.

"How's Sara?" He goes still at my question, looking up at me probably wondering how I knew he was married to his high school sweetheart. "Instagram."

Just because I hadn't talked to my brother doesn't mean that I didn't keep tabs on him. I also knew that they moved to Oahu through Instagram.

And Instagram is most likely the place that told him that I was at Duke.

"She's good, she is actually coming into town tomorrow morning." I nod.

We go back to sitting in awkward silence. When my phone vibrates on the table and I grab it to silence it, thinking it's Mason looking for me, when I see Alana calling.

Why is she calling this early? It's not even nine.

"What?" Aiden must notice something is off.

"Alana is calling." I feel my eyebrows bunching up.

"Okay?" He obviously doesn't see what is wrong with our stepmom calling this early.

"She wouldn't call this early. Something is up," I tell my brother before I press the green button on my screen.

"Alana?" I say into my phone and if I thought my world shattered last night, I was completely wrong.

CHAPTER TWENTY-SIX

Every text, every phone call keeps going unanswered, and I'm starting to get worried on top of being pissed off.

This morning I woke in Jordan's bed, alone. The only thing that told me not to look for her was the note that I found on her pillow. It said that she went to clear her head, so I got up and went home. I was going to let her clear her head as long as she needed to.

That was eight hours ago though. In the eight hours since I woke up, I haven't heard anything from her and I'm starting to get worried.

I try calling her phone one more time and yet again it gets sent to voice mail.

The frustration of it all finally gets to me because when I hear the sound of the beep for her voice mail, I slam my phone onto the kitchen table.

"Damn. What's your problem?" Carter comes into the kitchen and heads straight to the fridge.

"Have you heard from Jordan today?" My voice is filled with in agitation.

Carter raises his eyebrows at me, "No. I thought after

last night she would be in her room all day."

I let out a frustrated sigh, "Well, she's not. She left this morning before I woke up, leaving a note about needing to clear her head. I've haven't heard from her all day."

Carter scratches his chin, "Maybe she went to a meeting or something. Or maybe went to meet her sponsor or her probation officer."

Fuck. Why didn't I think of that? Why didn't I think that maybe she went to talk to someone about what happened last night? Someone that wasn't me?

Carter's suggestions make me relax a little bit. "That makes sense, but would it take all day?"

He shrugs. "Last night was a little tough for her."

That it was.

"Don't worry, man. I'm sure she will call soon." All I can do is nod. "You going to tell me how you know Aiden Garza?"

Carter pulls the chair next to me out, giving me a questioning look.

"I know him as Aiden Hall and I had no idea that he was Jordan's brother."

"I forget sometimes that he changed his last name." Carter shrugs. "So, you going to tell me?"

"Nothing to tell. Met the guy a few years back. He never went into detail about his family or his life before we met. Sure as hell don't remember ever meeting him before I was fifteen or sixteen."

"Weird shit." Carter muses.

"Tell me about it."

"Also, if I didn't love Jordan so much, I wouldn't have pulled you off him. Motherfucker deserved it." I can't help but partly agree with that statement.

The back door opens and I look up expecting it to be Jordan, but I let out a groan when Damon and Lucy walk in.

"Nice to see you too, jackass." Damon smirks, having heard my groan.

"I thought that you were Jordan." I slam my head against the table a few times.

"What's going on with Jordan?" I hear a chair getting pulled out so I'm guessing Lucy is taking a seat.

"I don't know, I haven't seen or heard from her all day." I say to the table.

"So? Just track her phone."

That grabs my attention. I look at Lucy and I give her a questioning look.

"Are you some sort of hacker that I don't know about?"

Girls can find guys in a matter of seconds on social media, so Lucy being a hacker wouldn't be far-fetched.

Lucy narrows her eyes at me like I'm crazy, "No. She has the FindMyFriends app on her phone, and you can track her location. You do have her on that app right?"

Now I'm looking at her like she's the crazy one, "No. Why would I?"

"Because you're her boyfriend and want to know where she is at all times?" She is talking about this like this is a normal thing to do.

"Do you track Damon wherever he goes?" Do people actually do that?

Lucy nods, "Yup and he can track me. I can track everyone in this house, actually. Including you."

"Okay, we are going to talk about the privacy issue later, but show me how you track her." I scoot closer to her.

Lucy rolls her eyes, "It's more of a location finder than a tracker." She pulls out her phone and opens the app that I've seen on my home screen. How she got my phone to install this app, I have no idea.

Her fingers swipe up until she reaches Jordan's name and clicks on it. Instantly the map on the screen changes from Duke University to a residential area.

"She's in Wilmington." Lucy holds out the phone for me to see. I take it to study the picture.

"Why would she go home without telling us? How did she even get there?" If she wanted to go home, she could have told me, and I would have taken her.

"She probably took the bus. If she went home she probably thought it would be a good idea to head to a place where her brother wouldn't be." Lucy shrugs again, like this is a normal occurrence.

"Where is Aiden anyway?" Damon asks, taking my attention from Lucy's phone.

"I have no idea, I haven't seen him since last night." I want to say that he is most likely at his hotel but I have no idea if that is true.

I spent all day worrying about Jordan, I forgot to call my friend and apologize for punching his face last night. I should do that.

A noise sounds through the kitchen, and Damon leans back to pull out his phone from his pocket.

"Hey Ma. What's up?" He answers. I've heard Damon talk to his mom on occasion, actually I've heard all of my roommates talk to their parents almost every other day.

I've even joined a few FaceTime calls with Jordan and her dad and on phone calls with Alana.

"We were just talking about her. None of us have

seen her all day, and I guess she's in Wilmington." Damon informs his mom, but why would she be asking about Jordan?

We all turn our eyes to Damon and something his mom is saying has him stiffening up and sitting up straight. The hairs on the back of my neck are standing up.

Something happened.

Before Damon can say another word, I pick up my phone and dial Jordan and again get sent to voice mail.

Damon clears his throat and finally speaks, "I'll tell them. Keep me posted?" His mom must have said something back because he nods. "Love you too, stay safe."

He ends the call and places it on the table. His face looks like he just seen a ghost.

"Babe, what's wrong? You're scaring me." Lucy reaches over to him and places a hand on his forearm.

"Um my mom said that they got word a few hours ago that a land mine had gone off at a US base in Afghanistan. The base that Jordan's dad was stationed at." He stops and swallows down hard. "There were a lot of casualties, but not all bodies were accounted for. As of this morning and still in effect fifteen minutes ago, Sergeant Major Garza has been reported missing in action until a body has been recovered."

A cold chill runs through my body.

That's why Jordan is in Wilmington. Alana must have called her and she went running.

I get up from the chair and I pocket my phone and head to the key hook at the front of the house and grab my keys.

"Where are you going?" Lucy follows me out of the kitchen as I grab my jacket.

"To Wilmington so that I can see with my own two eyes that Jordan is okay." My girl has been through a lot and I just know that she is getting destroyed by this.

"We're going with you," Lucy announces and I look at Carter and Damon behind her, they all nod.

"Are you sure?"

"She's our family, and I know a thing or two about a parent not coming home alive." Lucy's voice breaks and I know she is talking about her own dad. Fuck, this has to be bringing back painful memories for her.

"We'll pick up Gabe on the way." Carter swings the door open and practically runs out to the car.

Hold on, baby, we are coming to you.

CHAPTER TWENTY-SEVEN

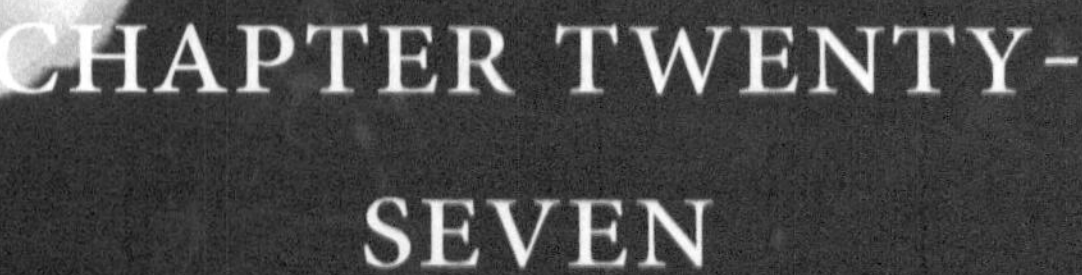

One of the biggest fears that a military family faces is getting that somber knock or phone call where you get notified that something has happened to your loved one.

Injured. Missing or the worst case scenario dead. There could be a number of things that could happen that will make the United State government utter the words, your soldier might not be coming home.

As a family, you have to prepare for that. You have to prepare for the possibility that you will get one of these notifications one day.

I prepared myself with my dad and did it again when Aiden enlisted. Even though I prepared myself for it, it doesn't mean that I accepted it.

When Alana called, she was in tears. She barely was able to get out the words that my dad was declared missing in action. Right away, Aiden called his supervisor for confirmation and when he had it we were in the car heading to Wilmington.

Getting to the house was the easy part, it was going to be a long road ahead waiting for any news.

They said that not all of the soldiers were accounted for, but that we should prepare ourselves for the worst.

We were told that we could get news in a few hours, a few days or the worst case scenario, a week or two.

Alana is already a mess, I don't know how she would be if she had to wait so fucking long for an ounce of news.

This wasn't supposed to happen. These last few weeks were supposed to be smooth sailing and then he would be home. This wasn't supposed to happen, he was supposed to be safe.

But I guess God had other plans. But when it comes to our family and my life, it seems like he always has other plans.

The first thing that I did when I got to my parents' house was check on Alana. She started crying the second she saw me and nearly fell to the ground. Once Aiden had a hold on her, I ran inside to check on Dylan. I found him in the living room staring at the phones on the coffee table, willing them to ring.

After a few hours of all of us sitting in the living room, not saying anything, I came up to my room. Then when I finally checked my phone and saw all the missed calls from Mason.

I should call him. I *need* to call him. Tell him everything that is going on, but I can't, not right now.

Not when I don't know anything and especially not when I have been drinking.

After the accident, my dad cleaned out all the alcohol out of the house. Well at least he thought he did. He forgot to check under the floorboards in my closet, where I had a stash. I didn't have a reason to take it out before but now I do.

I took out a bottle of tequila and now I'm currently sitting on my childhood room floor, with my door locked, drowning my sorrows.

My dad would hate me so much if he found me like this. If I'm being honest I hate myself.

I take another drink to feel the numbness.

When I was younger, when I felt the world around me crumbling down, I wished I had chosen something stronger than alcohol. Marijuana never helped, oxy was only a little fix, and unless I was constantly drinking, alcohol was a temporary effect. I think that's why I was drinking every single day, because the effect was only temporary.

If someone had died because of you, it wouldn't have been temporary.

Maybe I'll just drink more and more so I don't feel anything at all.

I always knew my limit when it came to drinking. I would only get to the point where I didn't feel the pain, yet still aware of the things happening around me. Never too far gone.

That isn't the case right now. I want to be so far gone that I don't have to feel the pain of losing yet another parent.

Because there is a high percent chance of that happening.

Just one more drink to let things go.

Everything is just one more.

* * *

It's hours later, and I must have fallen asleep because the room is dark and the night sky covers everything that I can see from my window.

There's a kink in my neck from falling asleep on the floor, and I'm sure my whole body is going to be sore for the next couple of days.

Sitting up, I try to stretch out my sore muscles as much as I possibly can. When all the kinks are somewhat gone, I just sit there in my dark room, in nothing but silence.

I reach for the bottle of tequila, but when I pick it up, it's empty. I must have finished it before falling asleep, which I have no recollection of.

Looks like a trip to the liquor store is in order.

Forcing myself to stand up, I sway a little until I get my balance. After a few seconds, I finally get my equilibrium back. Maybe tequila with no food in my system wasn't a good idea.

I make my way to my bedroom door, when I hear voices coming from downstairs. It sounds like too many people to just be Aiden, Alana and Dylan. Opening the door just a crack, I try to make out the voices and who they might belong to.

"Why are you here?" I know that voice. Why do I know that voice? It sounds like Mason, but he wouldn't be here, he's back at Duke.

"Because I was with her when Alana called and we drove over here as soon as she did." Aiden's voice is low and very much in control of the situation. I'm positive that if I were down there right now, I would be a blubbering mess.

"Why were you with her?" I swear that sounded so much like Carter. The tequila is playing tricks on me.

"Because she's my sister and I was trying to make things right." Is it just me or does he sound angry.

"You didn't seem to care much about her in years, so why now?" That voice sounds so much like Carter's. Maybe I need some water or some food. I should order a big greasy cheeseburger to soak up the alcohol. That would help.

I close the door, no longer caring what the voices are saying. The voices kept talking and talking for a few minutes, and then everything was quiet again.

Everything is quiet.

I hate when things are quiet.

But it's only quiet for a little bit, only until a phone rings downstairs. Then that's when the inner demons come out and play.

CHAPTER TWENTY-EIGHT

Three fucking days, that I haven't heard a word from Jordan.

I understand why I haven't heard from her, I do, but if I just received a single word text message from her, I will be okay. Not even that can I get to pop up on my screen.

On Friday night, Carter, Damon, Lucy and I went to pick up Gabe and went straight to Wilmington. The almost three hour ride was unbearable. I couldn't make my leg stop shaking the whole time. I was worried about Jordan and I wouldn't be okay until I saw her with my own two eyes.

When we got to the house and Aiden opened the door, I was a little taken aback. After hearing from Jordan everything that had gone down between them and with their dad, I never thought he would be there.

Yet he was.

Because he was with Jordan when she got the call from Alana.

I had so many questions, but at that moment I didn't care to ask them. All I wanted to do was to see Jordan, but Aiden said it wasn't the best time.

He told us that as soon as they knew something that

he would have her call us, or to even have her check in. He threw in the words. "Give her time."

Sorry if I was worried about how my girlfriend was handling the news of her dad being MIA.

The five of us left the house a little defeated but we stayed parked out front of the house for a few hours hoping that Jordan would pop out. She didn't

Sometime around one in the morning, we left Wilmington and I spent all day Saturday and yesterday waiting for a call from her.

A call that never came.

My phone didn't ring, no matter how many times I checked to see if it was working.

Now it's Monday, and I'm walking into the class that I share with Jordan, hoping that she's sitting in her seat, waiting for me. She isn't, much to my displeasure.

I let out a sigh when I walk into the classroom and see her empty chair.

Class goes on like everything is normal and at the end we turn in our project essays both electronically and on paper. It's a good thing that I had access to it otherwise without Jordan here, we would be screwed.

The professor asks us to fill out the form on the board so we can get a presentation schedule. When it's my turn, I hesitate, finally deciding on the last spot available for Monday. Hopefully Jordan is able to make it.

God, I wish she'll be here. Not only for the presentation but for my own sanity.

After leaving class, I get into my car and head home. The whole way to the house, I look to see if Jordan is walking somewhere on the sidewalk. I don't know why I do this to myself, I'm just setting myself up for more disappointment.

The second I'm inside the house, I dump all my crap on the floor and throw myself onto the couch.

"Rough day?" Gabe comes into the living room, dropping on the other side of the couch.

"Still haven't heard anything from Jordan," I grumble at him, closing my eyes hoping that if I close my eyes hard enough, maybe when I open them again she will be here next to me. Of course when I open them, that wish doesn't come true.

Gabe sighs. "Yeah, I had my grandma go over to her parents' house this morning to check on things. She said there was dead silence."

I turn to him. "You have your grandma doing stakeouts for you?" That has to be the weirdest thing that has ever come out of my mouth.

He shrug. "How else am I going to do it?"

It's something, I guess.

Throughout the next hour or so, Carter comes down from his room looking for food and Damon and Lucy come home from a date. Everyone somehow ends up in the living room, watching the ten o'clock news, wondering if today is the day we will see a news report about Jordan's dad.

Carter informed me that the military won't inform news outlets about a death until they notify the families. If we don't hear anything then it's most likely that nothing new has come out.

My phone vibrates in my pocket and I take it out right away, hoping that it might be Jordan finally reaching out.

When I look at the screen, all that hope disappears. It's my mom telling me that they are catching a redeye tonight into Jacksonville before making their way to Wilmington.

My parents would have been here sooner, had I told

them what was going on when I found out. But I'm a coward and held that information from them until this morning.

They jumped into action right away, wanting to be there for the Garza family as much as they can.

Great. My parents will get to see Jordan, but I won't. Maybe with them there, she will finally respond to my texts.

I don't really know what happens after that, I must have dozed off because I jolt up when I hear someone banging on the door.

Looking around the living room, everyone looks surprised that there is someone pounding on our door at this hour.

"What's going on?" Lucy cuddles closer into Damon's chest, fear present in her face.

"I don't know." Carter gets up and heads to the door as another pound sounds. "What the fuck?"

As Carter opens the door, it swings open, Aiden and Dylan barreling in. Instantly I'm on my feet.

"Is she here?" Aiden looks like he hasn't slept in days and has a manic look to his face.

"Who's here?" It might be a dumb question on Gabe's part.

"Dani!" Aiden yells out and we all go on high alert.

"She's not here. Why would she be here?" I try to keep my tone as calm as I can before something erupts in me and I move the whole fucking world for this girl.

"Because I went to go check on her a few hours ago and she wasn't there." Dylan runs a hand through his hair, nearly pulling it out in frustration.

"Where the fuck would she go?" I feel as if my teeth are going to break by how hard my jaw is set.

Dylan shakes his head, "I don't know, she's not

answering her phone. She's been in her room since Friday and has only come out a couple of times."

"She's been drinking." Aiden rubs a hand across his face, and when he pulls it away he looks like he is ready to let out a sob. "I found more than a few empty bottles in her room."

"Fuck!" I yell out, scaring everyone. I start pacing thinking of places where she would go. Then I remember how we found her in Wilmington, "Check your app." I turn to Lucy abruptly and I startle her.

After a few seconds, she is able to compose herself and pulls out her phone.

Her eyebrows bunch up and her lips purse, "It says her location is the dorm."

Without thinking twice, I grab my keys and run out the door, hearing footsteps behind me. I get into my car and Carter gets into the passenger seat. As I pull out of the driveway, I see Aiden and Dylan pulling out behind me.

I don't know how but we make it to Jordan and Lucy's building in five minutes. It's past curfew but I learned a trick last week on how to get into the building without having someone come down. The good ole credit card in the door slot trick.

Once I have the door open, the four of us charge in running up to Jordan's floor.

Please be here.

Please be here.

I chant the whole way up to her floor and as we make our way to her room, I pray that she's okay.

If she has been drinking, I have no clue what we will be walking into.

As soon as we reach her door, I pound as hard as I

can.

"Jordan! Are you in there?" I wait to hear a sound, but nothing comes from the other side.

"Baby, please open the door!" I pound my fist again against the thick wooden door and still nothing.

"She has to be in there. Where else would she be?" Dylan has fear in his voice and that's what drives my decision.

"Fuck it, I'm breaking down the door."

Jordan lives in the upperclassmen dorm rooms, there is no RA to ask for a key.

Breaking down the door is our only option.

"Do it." Aiden encourages. They all stand back and I'm about to charge at the door, when I hear Lucy scream.

"I have the key!" I stop where I'm standing, as I watch Lucy wave her keys around.

Her, Damon and Gabe must have followed us and just arrived.

In the moment of all the worry, I completely forgot about Jordan and Lucy being roommates.

Lucy being here is getting us closer to Jordan.

She opens the door and once she turns the nob I charge.

I run in, and I feel my heart sink.

Jordan is on her bed, laying on her back, with a bottle of Jack on the floor, her arms outstretched for it. As I get closer, I see that there is something coming from her mouth.

Vomit.

No. No. No. No!

Running straight to her, I try to shake her as gently as I can.

"Baby? Can you hear me? Jordan, please answer me,

sweetheart?"

I hear a sob and it takes me a second to realize it's coming from me.

I push her hair back, sliding my hand down her face until I reach her pulse point. I feel a thump. Its light but it's there

"She still has a pulse." Without another thought I lift her in my arms and head for the door.

"We gotta get her to University hospital." Aiden yells next to me, guiding me down the stairs.

We have to hurry because we might be too late.

Hold on, baby. *Please* hold on.

CHAPTER TWENTY-NINE

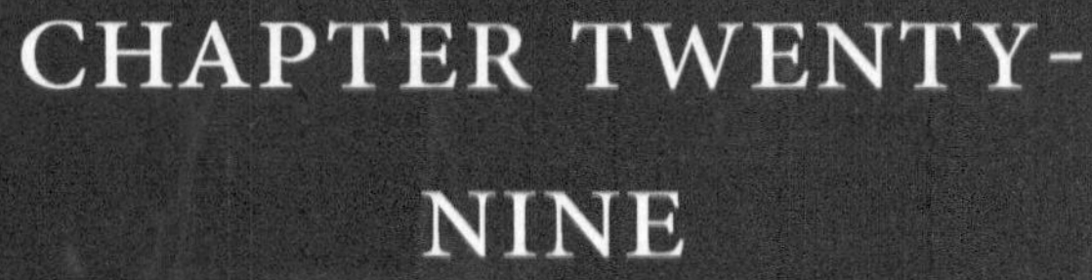

My eyes feel like they have sand poured in them. They are probably bright red and the only thing that will help at this point is a whole day of sleep.

Sleep that I won't get until Jordan is awake and out of the hospital.

We got her to the emergency room in time according to the nurses. The vomit at the edge of her mouth was fresh and if we had found her any later, she could have choked on her own vomit and it could have been deadly.

In the car, I put her on her side trying to get as much of it out of her mouth before it could get to that point.

They are treating Jordan for alcohol poisoning and pumped her stomach as soon as her throat was cleared.

That was six hours ago. They're keeping her for observation to make sure that she doesn't have any permanent damage. The nurse told us that there are cases where alcohol poisoning can cause parts of the brain to shut down. They are hoping that isn't the case.

"We got a phone call. That's why Dylan went to check

on her, so that she could come down and we could tell her that they found Dad." Aiden's words are like a bucket of ice water.

"They found him?" There are so many ways that this could go.

He nods. "They found him. Somehow he was buried under a pile of combusted metal. They flew him to the VA hospital in Germany."

"He's alive?" Please tell me I'm hearing this correctly.

"He's alive. I don't know how." Aiden's voice breaks slightly. "He had a pulse when they found him and he was in stable condition when he arrived in Germany. They held off on telling us because they didn't know if he was going to make it."

From where I'm sitting, I can see that it's taking a lot for Aiden not to break down. He may be a military man, but he could have lost two people he loves in a span of a few days.

"Do you think that they would let us see her yet?" I ask, trying to distract him a little.

He looks over at the nurses' station. "Probably not."

It's after visitation hours or before since its almost six in the morning. Jordan has been admitted and the nurses were strict with telling us that we couldn't see her until the morning. The only one that could go in was Alana.

Alana showed up a few hours ago with Sara, Aiden's wife, at her side. Alana went straight to Dylan and Aiden before marching to the nurses' station and started demanding that she see her daughter. I guess she scared them because soon after, they were escorting her back.

That's where she is right now, with Jordan. Where I so desperately want to be.

I look around the waiting room and see a handful of tired faces.

Lucy, Damon and Gabe arrived a little bit after we did.

Sara is sitting in between Aiden and Dylan, holding each of their hands, comforting them. On my right are my parents. They had just gotten on their flight when all of this started to go down, so when they landed I called them and told them what happened and they drove over here.

It was a long night but I don't think that any of us will be getting any sleep until we know Jordan is going to be okay, and see her with our own eyes.

Well at least until I do.

So much has happened in these last couple of days. There are so many things that I would have done differently. For one, I would have fought Jordan a lot harder about drinking at the party. I should have fought to keep her away from the party.

What kind of person puts their girlfriend in harm's way like that? Apparently I do.

I should have been more vigilant with her. I should have done everything in my power to not let it get to this point.

Sometime around seven forty-five in the morning, Alana finally comes out to the waiting room and I jump up to my feet.

"Is she okay?" The question was fast, I have no idea how she understood me but she did.

Alana nods. Her eyes are red and puffy telling me that she was crying all night, "She is. She should be released in a couple hours and then will be under my supervision for the next twenty four."

I nod. "Can I see her?"

I need to see my girl. I need to see if she's okay. I need to feel her hand in mine.

Alana nods again, "I think she would like that." She walks me to the room but doesn't go make a move to go in with me.

A small hand lands on my forearm. "Thank you Mason. If you hadn't rushed over, I don't know if she would be here."

I swallow down the lump in my throat that is forming with just the thought of not having Jordan here with me.

"Of course," I tell her.

"I know you love her. I'm glad that she found someone that really cares about her." With a small smile, Alana turns and walks back to the waiting room, leaving me alone to see what is waiting for me behind this door.

Taking a deep breath, I push the door open and I feel like my heart starts to beat again when my eyes land on Jordan.

Her skin looks pale and not the caramel color I love so much. She is wearing a hospital gown, and she has a few blankets covering her lower half. Her hair looks like a knotted mess but still looks beautiful. There is an IV in her left arm and some oxygen tubes in her nostrils. She looks peaceful

I move deeper into the room, going straight to her bedside. I brush a few pieces of hair out of her face before planting a kiss on her temple.

Pulling the vacant chair closer to her side, I take a seat, taking her hand in mine.

It feels so fragile and so much smaller than mine. Jordan has always been this big ball of something whenever she is near me, never feeling small compared to my six-foot-five frame.

Now it feels like if I hold her hand too tight it might break.

"I was so scared, baby." I press my lips against her hand. "For a second, I thought that I had lost you. It fucking wrecked me seeing you like that." I may never get that image of Jordan out of my head, no matter how hard I try.

Jordan doesn't stir, her body is completely still and if I didn't know any better I would say that was gone.

But she's not.

She's here because I was able to get to her in time.

I press my lips to her hand, harder than I did earlier as if I could brand her with my lips.

"There are a lot of things that I should have done when it comes to you, but I should have protected you more than anything." I swallow through the lump in my throat.

"I don't know what I would have done if I had lost you." She can't hear the words, but I will keep saying them however long I need to.

"Because I fucking love you. So, so much, Jordan."

Those words she should be hearing when she's awake, laughing and smiling. Not in a hospital bed recovering from alcohol poisoning.

I sit next to her for however long as I can, still with her hand wrapped around mine. The nurses come in and out to check on her frequently and when I ask if it's normal to sleep this much, apparently it is.

At almost ten o'clock, the hand that's in mine starts to flex a little.

Looking up, I see that Jordan still has her eyes closed but her face is all scrunched up as if she was in pain.

"Hey." I stand up and brush her hair back trying to soothe her as best as I can.

Those brown eyes that I love so much, slowly open up and stare back at me with so many questions floating in them.

"Wh-what happened?" Her words stutter a little bit and I can clearly hear just how scared she is.

I let out a sigh and caress her cheek, "You ended up drinking too much, and got alcohol poisoning. They had to pump your stomach and are keeping you for observation to make sure you didn't suffer any brain damage or anything."

She stares up at me as if the words I'm saying are in a different language.

"We were able to get to you in time." I try to give her a smile but it comes out small and doesn't reach my eyes.

Jordan just nods and her eyes shift to the room surrounding us.

It's a plain hospital room with machines and a smell that will probably stay attached to our clothes for a while.

I have questions but I don't want to push her, especially not after everything that she has been through. But I have to put those feelings aside and get the answers I need.

"When did you get back to campus, Jordan?"

Her eyes fly to mine instantly. There is a look on her face that I can't really get a read on. It's like a mixture of confusion and anger.

"Jordan," I prompt her.

She closes her eyes and lets out a sigh, "Sometime around noon. I couldn't be in the house anymore just waiting for the phone to ring. I needed to get out. So I got on the bus and came to campus."

This girl must be fucking ninja if she left the house

undetected and not have them notice until hours later.

"Do you remember how much you had to drink?" I should stop with the questions. It feels like I have her under interrogation. I can't help but wonder how she must feel.

She shakes her head. "I know I drank Friday and Saturday, but was dry on Sunday. It had only been a few hours and I was going crazy about finding my next drink. I think that's why I came back to school, I just don't remember anything after getting off the bus."

A part of me wants to yell at her, to yell that she should have come to me, maybe then we wouldn't be here.

I hold it in.

I hold it in, and all I do is nod and press my lips against her forehead. "I thought I lost you. Seeing you like that." I pause trying to get my bearings right, "I thought that was it. I wasn't going to ever see your eyes opening again."

I press my lips to hers and a chaste kiss and when I pull back, I see tears forming in her eyes.

"Are you okay?" I think she can hear the concern in my voice.

She shakes her head. "You need to leave Mason."

Pretty sure, I now know what it feels like for your heart to break.

"Do you not want me here?" My eyebrows bunch up. Maybe she wants to see Alana or her brothers, maybe that's why she's telling me to leave.

Yet another head shake. "You have your whole life ahead of you. You don't need someone like me holding you down. You deserve someone to give you the world, not someone who is broken and has no way to be repaired."

"Baby," I start but she just keeps shaking her head making me stop.

"I've never gone this far. Yes, I've been in a car accident. I've blacked out, sure, but never have I been on the brink of death like this. What if it happens again? What if I can't get the help that I need and it happens again, but that time it's too late? I can't do that to you. I will never do that to you. So you need to leave while you still can and move on."

There are tears running down her face now. I just want to reach over and wipe them away.

"I told you that I will be by your side through anything. Let me be there for you through this."

"You need to leave." A sob escapes her lips when she says the words and my heart breaks even more.

"Jordan."

"No, Mason. Please leave. Move on, forget about me. Find someone who doesn't live a shattered life. Just please, go."

There is pain in her eyes, that much I can tell. I just don't know if the pain is there because she hates what she is telling or for something else.

This is something that I should fight her on. I should be putting my foot down and tell her that I'm not going anywhere.

But I can't find it in me to do it.

If this is what she wants, then I will give it to her. Because I love her, she has become my whole world and if I have to walk away from that, I will.

I nod, taking a step back from her. "I'll go get Alana, I'm sure she wants to see you."

Another sob escapes her lips as she nods.

With one last look at the woman I love, I walk out of the room.

When I walk back into the waiting room, all eyes turn to me and I try my hardest not to show my heart on my sleeve.

"She's awake." I give the room a smile but I'm sure that some can see it's forced.

Right away, Alana, Aiden and Dylan stand up and head to the room.

I tell my parents that I'm going to head home real quick, and that I'll meet up with them later.

Not looking back, I head out of the hospital.

Jordan is not broken, and I need to find a way to show her that.

CHAPTER THIRTY

Jordan

The darkness almost swallowed me whole. I also almost let the broken pieces of my past dig into each and every one of my organs and let them take over.

The darkness and the brokenness were too much for me to handle, so I let them have their way. I let them dictate how I should run my life.

It was only for a few days that they took over, but it's those few days that nearly destroyed everything.

Only a few days and my life was almost gone.

And I have nobody to blame but myself.

Everything I did in those few days is all my fault.

I was released from the hospital yesterday afternoon. After a lot of test, the doctor said it was okay for me to go home, but I had to be under supervision for at least twenty-four hours.

So as soon as I got released, Alana got a room at the hotel Aiden was staying at last week, before deciding to drive back to Wilmington today. Of course with me in tow.

This woman has been through hell these last few days and I just added to it. I will be forever grateful for her, and forever repaying my dues.

When we got to the hotel room yesterday afternoon, she told me the news about my dad. The news that said that he was found alive and is currently in a hospital in Germany recovering.

I cried the whole night.

My dad is alive and will be coming home soon and if things had gone differently on Monday, I wouldn't have been here to see him.

I would be in an icebox instead of in the car with Alana and Dylan, heading to my childhood home.

And the only reason that I'm here is because of Mason.

Dylan told me what he did, how he reacted right away when he and Aiden went to look for me at the house. Mason jumped straight into action and went to my dorm to look for me. He was the one that saw me first and he was the one that held me when they drove me to the hospital.

Mason saved me and the way I repaid him was by telling him to leave.

It broke me even more when I saw the look of pain on his face, that I wanted to take back everything that I said right away. But I couldn't.

I've put Mason through too much, everything from keeping things from him, to not telling him the whole truth and now this. He shouldn't be with me, I'm way too toxic and completely unfixable to be a person who owns his heart. So I let him go, so that he could live the best life he could and be with someone that will hold his heart near and never crush it.

Mason Hawke deserves the world and I shouldn't get in the way of that.

Alana takes the exit for Wilmington and soon she

is pulling into our driveway. Once the car is in park, she doesn't make a move to get out, she just sits there looking at the garage door.

I know what's coming and just thinking about it causes tears to spring in my eyes.

"Before we go into the house, I need to know if you're hiding any more alcohol." Her voice is stern and a little cold.

I shake my head, "No." My voice is raspy and the fact that I have a baseball sized lump in my throat doesn't help either. "There isn't any more alcohol hidden."

Because I drank it all, but I didn't tell her that.

She nods. "I understand why you did it, Jordan. I do. I get why you took a drink at the party Thursday night, and I understand why you felt the need to drink on Friday."

I look at her incredulously. How does she know I drank on Thursday?

It's as if she heard my silent question because she turns to me, eyebrows raised. "Aiden told me. He told me while we were in the waiting room."

I just nod. What else is there to do?

"You're twenty-one. You are out in the real world, on your own, so I know that I don't have the liberty to tell you what to do. But the shit that happened on Monday, cannot happen again. If you don't give a shit about what other people will go through if you do that again, then you will get out of this car and you will be on your own. Because I will not let my family go through that again. If I have to see my daughter walk away, then so be it, but I will not watch her die right in front of me."

The sob that she has been holding in, finally escapes and I let mine loose the second I see my stepmother break down.

Alana could have walked away when my father told her that he had kids. She could have told him that she didn't want that responsibility. She was in her mid-twenties and she had every right to walk away, but she didn't. She accepted her boyfriend's kids with open arms and treated us as her own in the years that came and went. I almost selfishly took away a child from her, not only once but twice with my latest stunt.

I deserve each and every one of her words.

"I'm going to get help, I promise. I will get help and I will make sure this doesn't happen again." I cry out, a pain in my chest making it unbearable.

"How, Jordan? How will you do that?" Alana powers through the tears.

"I don't know, but I will figure it out and I will regain your trust somehow." I wipe the tears from my face already thinking of ways that I can go about this. The first call is to my sponsor, the next to my probation officer.

"It's not that you lost my trust Jordan." Alana's voice is softer "It's that I'm scared that we are going to lose you, and this family will not be able to handle that." Her hand lands on my forearm, and she gives me a look of sadness.

"You won't lose me. I promise that I will get help," I tell her and then I remember that Dylan is still in the car, so I reach around and extend my hand to him. He takes it and gives it a reassuring squeeze. "It won't be easy for me and I probably won't do it alone, but I promise that I won't do this again. I won't put you in another situation where you're scared for my life. I promise."

And I'm keeping my promise this time. I can't put my family through this again.

Dylan nods and so does Alana. After a few minutes,

we are all calm and collected and are able to get out of the car and into the house.

We spend the rest of the afternoon and night watching movies and eating pizza. Sara and Aiden joined us too and it was like we were a happy family again. Even if we aren't, because my dad is not here and I put my family through hell wondering if I was going to pull through.

Such an amazing daughter and sister I am.

That night, I can't sleep. I keep tossing and turning and once I feel I will get a good few hours in, I wake up.

I give up trying to find sleep around six in the morning. Without putting much thought into it, I get dressed in running shorts and shoes, and reach for a hoodie. The fabric color catches my eye and I realize that it's Mason's.

I came home for Easter weekend and he came with me. We ended up having a bonfire at the beach that weekend and he gave me his hoodie to wear. I never gave it back to him.

Without thinking, I throw it on, head downstairs to leave a note for Alana and head out the door for a run.

Running isn't something that I usually do, and I probably shouldn't, given that I was lying in a hospital bed a few days ago getting my stomach pumped, it's definitely not a good idea. But I need something to clear my head, and right now I will take anything.

So I chose exercise since I can't really eat anything solid.

I don't run very far. I'm lucky enough that my parents' house is about twenty minutes away from the shore.

Growing up, the sound of the water hitting the shore has always had a calming effect on me. Coming to the beach and seeing the sand and the dark water was my saving grace.

I make my way to the sand and because it's so early in the morning there is nobody here, leaving me the beach all to myself. The Atlantic Ocean and all.

Plopping down in the middle of everything, I bring my knees up to my chest and just watch as the water crashes into the sand. I sit there in silence and try to clear my head as best I can.

I hear the footsteps about fifteen minutes into sitting in the quietness. Figured he would show up sooner or later, since when I ran by his dad's house, his car was in the driveway. Either he was keeping a lookout for me to pass by his house or he was tracking me through that app that Lucy put on my phone.

I'm going with the app.

He comes up next to me and instantly lets his ass fall to the ground. It's several minutes before he breaks the silence.

"I had money on you being out here later in the morning, not at six," Carter's voice rings over the crashing waves.

"I couldn't sleep." I keep my gaze straight ahead instead of turning to my best friend.

"Understandable. Given everything that has been going on the last week or so." It's a little crazy how things have shifted in just a few days. Last week at this time, I was happy, sleeping in Mason's arms. A few hours later everything turned to shit.

"You didn't have to come." When we were teenagers, Carter got into the habit of always being there when I needed him to be. Whether it was my first kiss, when I wanted someone to vent to or just to sit in silence, he was always at my side. Him being here is no surprise to me.

"No, but what kind of best friend would I be if I didn't come to the beach with you at six o'clock in the morning? You can get attacked by a seagull or something."

I turn to him and he gives me a boyish grin.

"Are you here to lecture me?" I narrow my eyes at him.

He shakes his head. "I just wanted to spend time with my best friend." The way he says the words makes me want to cry.

"I'm sorry." I don't have to voice why I'm apologizing. He already knows.

"Don't do it again, okay? I can't lose my sister."

The tears finally escape at his words. Fuck, I'm a selfish bitch.

Carter wraps an arm around my shoulders and I cry into his chest. I cry even harder when I realize that I want a certain set of arms wrapped around me and I told him to leave.

"I'm going to see if Duke has any resources for this kind of thing." I sniffle, wiping the snot coming from my nose with the sleeve of the hoodie. Great, now Mason's hoodie has boogers.

I can feel him nod against my hair. "Whatever you want to do, I'll be your friend through all of it. Your brother. Whatever."

Now I'm the one nodding against him.

We sit in silence for a little while and once again, Carter is the one breaking the silence.

"Don't end it with Mason." This has me pulling back. I'm guessing that he must have figured out that something happened between us if he's bringing it up.

I shake my head and let out a sig. "It's for the best. He deserves a lot more than what I can give him."

"And what can't you give him?" Carter raises an eyebrow.

"Um, stability? I kept things from him, I have a lot of dark shit in my life. He doesn't need that." I can go on with what I can't give Mason.

"Okay that's just crap. Up until a few days ago, you were good. So you had a lapse in judgement. We all do because we are all human. Just because that happened doesn't mean that you are not stable. You're one of the most stable people I know. You were around people who drank for two and a half years and not once did you have a drink. As for keeping things from him, yeah that is true, but if you look at it he doesn't seem to care about that very much. And yes, you have a dark past, but just because the past is dark, doesn't mean that future will be."

I thought we said no lectures. Instead of keeping my eyes on him, I turn back to the water.

"You're afraid." It's not a question.

"I don't know what you're talking about."

"Yeah you do. You're afraid that if you get close to Mason, he's going to leave just like Aiden did. That you're going to do something and he's going to walk." I shake my head, more tears threatening to spill out.

"No."

"Then why Jordan? Tell me why your boyfriend is moping around the house like he just got his heart ripped out." His words sting a little. I didn't want Mason to be mopping, I thought that he would bounce back quickly.

"Because what if I do something else that I regret?

What if another accident happens and this time whoever is with me doesn't make it? Or what if what happened on Monday wasn't a fluke and it happens again but this time it's too late?" I won't put Mason through that, not if I have a say.

"But what if those things don't happen? You are going to make yourself unhappy because of a hypothetical?"

Why does he have to come here and have me second guess my decision?

"I'm a broken girl that doesn't deserve to be repaired." I'm acting like a petulant child right now but if it's the only way to get my point across, so be it.

"You have to stop putting all the guilt on yourself. Damon and Dylan have forgiven you, so has everyone else, but when are you going to forgive yourself?"

"Forgiving myself means that it didn't happen. It did happen and I should be held accountable for my actions." Nearly killing two people should not be forgiven so easily.

"You were held accountable but you still torture yourself with it."

He's right, of course he's right.

Carter wraps his arm around me again.

"Mason is good for you. You're good for him. Seeing you together made me worry less about you, because I know he will be there for you no matter what and that he will protect you and love you always. You just have to let him."

You just have to let him.

What if I can't?

What if it's too late and he doesn't want anything to do with me?

CHAPTER THIRTY- ONE

Night classes have become the bane of my existence and I want nothing to do with them anymore. Especially ones that remind me of Jordan.

It's been one week. One week since we rushed Jordan to the hospital for alcohol poisoning, and it has been six days since she told me to leave her side.

It has taken everything in me to not drive the two, almost three hours to Wilmington to park in front of her parents and wait for her to come out. But I refrained. Same thing with sending text messages and calling.

She wanted me to leave, so I'm giving her what she wanted.

I don't fucking like it but I'm doing it.

Baseball served as a distraction for a few days, since there was an away game but once I got home it was back to thinking about her.

It also doesn't help that today is the big presentation for our class and her not being here means we lose half a grade.

In all honestly, I'd rather lose half a grade than force

Jordan to be here.

Unlike last Monday, I don't look for Jordan wh walk into class. She isn't going to be here, there is no need for me to get my hopes up thinking I might see her.

I make my way to my unassigned seat and I start to get everything ready to do this presentation, alone.

A few minutes before the professor starts the class, the chair next to me gets pulled out.

Automatically, my attention goes to the chair. Whoever is pulling that chair and taking a seat has some fucking balls. Just because Jordan is not here doesn't mean that I want anyone to sit next to me.

My eyes travel to the person and my jaw nearly drops to the floor.

Her brown hair is down and in waves, flowing down her back. Her face looks thinner than it did last week and she has dark circles under her eyes that tell me that she hasn't been sleeping.

My eyes travel from her face down her body, and I notice that she is wearing one of my baseball hoodies and jeans that fit her body perfectly.

For sure my eyes are playing tricks on me, because no way in hell is Jordan taking a seat next to me. To confirm that she is real, my stupid hand slowly makes its way to her thigh that is inches from mine, and pokes her.

Shit. I just actually did that, didn't I?

She gives me a weird look before shaking her head and turns her attention to the front of the classroom.

Jordan is really here. She's here and she has yet to say a word to me.

"I wasn't going to let you fail." Her voice is a simple whisper that jolts something inside of me.

Our professor sent out the presentation schedule on Thursday morning for everyone in the class. A part of me hoped that Jordan would see it and show up. It was a small part, but as Monday got closer I gave up on it. She wasn't going to show up, but yet she proved me wrong and she is here.

I don't respond to her comment, I just give her a nod and turn my attention back to the front, mentally preparing myself for the presentation.

At least, that's what I should be doing. I should be mentally preparing myself for our presentation and learning something from the others, but all my attention is on the girl next to me.

All week, I tried my hardest to not think of her. The only time I let myself have that luxury was when Carter came home after spending a few days in Wilmington and told me she was okay. I wanted to believe him, that she really was okay, but I needed to see it with my own eyes.

Do I believe him now? Possibly, but from what I can see, she looks okay but she may have a ways to go to get to where she was before.

I still can't get over the fact that she is wearing my hoodie. What does it mean? Is she trying to tell me something? Are we even still together at this point?

Shaking my head, I try my hardest to listen to what my classmates are saying in their presentations.

The time continues to tick by and soon, the second to last presentation goes and then it's mine and Jordan's turn.

I direct her to the front of the class and once we are settled, we start.

Our topic for this assignment was episodic memory, which is basically our own personal memory and how we remember those memories.

We work through the presentation flawlessly, no mistakes, no stumbles and plenty of eye contact with the audience.

Once we are finished, we stand there waiting for questions from the professor.

"Is there something that you two remember in this type of way, something recently or from your childhood?"

It's a simple question but for one of us the answer can be complicated.

I look at Jordan but she is looking at the professor with a blank expression, so I answer.

"My first baseball game. I remember it as one of the best days of my life, my mom remembers it as me sitting on the bench the whole time." It's simple and it goes with the assignment.

Professor Jones nods, "What about you Jordan? Any episodic memories that stick out?"

Jordan nods at him. "I have quite a few actually, but I think that the one that sticks out is the one that happened most recently." I watch her as her eyes leave Professor Jones and then turn to me quickly before turning back. "Last week, something happened where I had to be rushed to the hospital. I don't remember a whole lot but the one thing I do remember is seeing my boyfriend's face when I came to. He might remember it differently, but I remember seeing so much concern on his face that I wanted to figure out a way to make it go away."

Fuck.

I remember thinking that she was scared and confused, never worried about me.

"Thank you for sharing that with us, Jordan, that

experience must have left a lasting impression on you," Professor Jones says to her and she just nods.

"Great job, you two." We get dismissed and head back to our seats. Class continues on for the next few minutes, Professor Jones tells us when to expect grades and dismisses us.

The whole time that I'm packing up my things, I'm very aware of Jordan and every move she makes.

When all her stuff is collected, she stands at her full height and gives me a tentative smile before she turns and starts walking out of the room.

Am I really going to just watch her walk away?

No, fuck that.

I'm tired of all the silence.

Catching up to her, I walk a few steps behind her until we reach the parking lot, then I grab her by the elbow and stop her

"Wait." My fingers flex around her elbow and I try my hardest not to pull her to me. My body is silently crying for hers.

Jordan's eyes are a little wide and her lips are parted. All I want to do is lean in and claim her mouth for all to see. So the whole fucking campus could know that she belongs to me and I to her.

"Can we go somewhere to talk?" My thumb rubs against the cloth covering her elbow. She stares up at me for a few seconds before she nods.

"We can go back to my dorm room, if you'd like?" She gives me a small smile, but my mind is somewhere else.

Her dorm room.

The room that I broke down the door so that I could get to her. The room she was passed out in and if I was even a few minutes later, I would have lost her.

She must sense my hesitation because her hand lands on my forearm and she gives it a reassuring squeeze.

"Aiden and Dylan cleaned it out before I went back. It's fine." She gives me a reassuring smile. After taking a few seconds to think it over, I give her a nod.

Without a second thought from her, we make our way to her dorm room.

I almost lost her once in that room.

Will I lose her again?

I guess I'm about to find out.

CHAPTER THIRTY-TWO

When Jordan said that her brothers cleaned it out, she meant that they took everything out of the room, leaving her only with the two beds and desk.

As soon as I walk in, I look at her for an explanation.

"I'm moving. Not schools, just to an apartment closer to the house. Alana found it last week and I rented it out right away. It's a three-bedroom, and Lucy is moving in and then Dylan, when he comes in the fall." She places her backpack on the desk, waving me to take a seat on the bed.

"Why?" It's a stupid question, because I may already know the answer.

"I don't want to be surrounded by bad memories all the time. So when Alana brought it up, I agreed." She shrugs like this is one of the simplest things in the world.

A part of me wants to say to her that I would move in with her and Lucy could take my room or maybe Dylan, but I don't think we are there.

"I think that this would be good for you." And it will be, if she is on the right path, she can conquer anything.

"Me too." She gives me a tentative smile, like she is unsure of what to do next.

"Look…"

"Mason…"

We both start to speak at the same time. I can't help but smile when she lets out a little giggle at the mix up.

"You go first." I wave to her, staying seated on the bed as she comes to stand in front of me.

"Mason, I'm sorry. Kicking you out of the hospital was the worst possible thing that I could do. If it wasn't for you running over here, things could have been a lot worse. I should have thanked you for taking me to the hospital and for being there in the hospital with me. Instead, I told you to leave." Her chin quivers and she bows her head.

I can hear it in her voice that asking me to leave hurt her just as much as it did me.

Standing up from the bed, I step closer to her, placing my forefinger and thumb under her chin.

"Can I ask you why you did it?"

Her brown eyes, coated in tears look at me and I hear her swallow audibly.

"Because you deserve someone that isn't as broken as me. That doesn't come with all the baggage that I carry." A tear slips from her eye and I swipe it away with my thumb.

"You keep saying that. That you're broken, but I don't see you as broken. I see a gorgeous, sexy as hell woman that is learning how to navigate life and hit a few bumps along the way." I move my hand from her chin to cradling her face. "I never saw you as broken and I never will. I love you just the way you are."

Her eyes go wide at my words.

Words that I've only gotten to say while she was

unconscious.

Words that I've been wanting to say to her for a little while now, but didn't have the courage to do so. I told her at the hospital, but that doesn't count. She wasn't awake to hear them.

"Wh-What did you say?" She's all flustered by my declaration. It's cute.

"I said, I love you just the way you are." I give her a smile. "I love you Jordan. I really, truly do."

The tears that were coating her eyes earlier finally escape, a little too quickly for me to wipe away.

Not that she would give me a chance to wipe them away, because her lips cover mine before I can make a move.

My body takes a few seconds to figure out what exactly is going on, but as soon as it does, my arms are wrapping around Jordan's waist bringing her closer to me.

I grip her waist tightly, lifting her up and prompting her legs to wrap around my waist. Her arms go around my neck and her fingers go straight to my hair, pulling it just the way I like it.

I'm about to slide my tongue along her bottom lip to ask for access when she pulls back from me. The sadness and tears that coated her eyes earlier are gone and in its place are want, need and lust. In that fucking order.

Fuck. She looks so beautiful looking at me with those bedroom eyes. I'm so fucking gone for this girl, I never want to go back to a time where I wasn't.

"I love you too. That's why I pushed you away because I love you and I wanted you to be happy." Her breath dances against my face, her words prompting a growl to escape.

"I am happy. With you. And if you ever think otherwise again, I will lay you across my knee and show you just how happy you make me." Somehow that sounded sexier in my head than it did coming out of my mouth.

Jordan's eyebrows raise in a challenge. "Never been into spanking all that much, but with you, I'd try. Maybe we can even do some exploration into anal play. If you're up for it." The smile that is on her lips is sweet but her words are anything but. Hearing her say that she would try anything with me makes my cock swell up even more.

"As long as it's me claiming this luscious ass of yours, then I'm golden, baby." I plant my lips on hers again, before she pulls back again.

Her eyes still have lust swimming in them but there is also something serious floating around.

"I really am sorry, Mason. Hopefully one day I will be able to forgive myself for my actions of the last week. Until I do, I will apologize every single day, even when you don't want to hear it."

This girl.

"If it means having you by my side for the rest of my life then I will hear those words till the day I die." The words are like a whisper against her lips. I can already taste her on my tongue and I want more.

"Forever?"

"Forever."

My lips find their salvation when they meet Jordan. Hiking her up more, I grab onto her globes and hold her tight as I grind her pussy against my jean clad cock.

Jordan moans against my mouth and this time when I slide my tongue along the seam of her bottom lip, she doesn't pull away.

My tongue dances with hers and I tongue fuck her mouth just like I plan to do with her sweet cunt.

"Mason." I fucking love when she say my name like that, all raspy and full of need and sex.

I dig my fingers deeper into the cheeks of her ass, possibly making holes in her leggings.

"What do you want, baby? Tell me."

"Clothes. Off."

What my girl asks for, she shall receive.

Turning, I drop Jordan onto her bed and drag her to the end of it, pulling her leggings right off,. Her giggle filling the room.

"I fucking missed that giggle." I groan out when I see that she is wearing one of her flimsy thongs that doesn't cover anything, making my mouth water.

While I'm ogling her barely covered pussy, she sits up and throws off my hoodie, then follows with her shirt and bra.

I'm going to die of blue balls if I don't get my cock inside her of my mouth or her cunt that is getting wetter by the second.

"Your turn." The words barely leave her mouth when I'm already pulling at the fabrics covering my body. I feel like a teenage boy that has only seen porn once and is about to get with the girl of his dreams.

And that's what Jordan is, the girl of my dreams.

The second my dick is out of its restraints it bounces off my stomach, asking for attention. The tip is already starting to turn purple and if I don't get any friction soon, I will be dying of blue balls at the ripe age of twenty one.

"Mm looks like you may need a little help with that." Jordan's hand lands on my shaft, and I throw my head back in pleasure. She gives me a few good strokes before she goes lower and cups my balls, pulling them, squeezing them in her small hands.

I'm about to lose it when she licks the vein that runs up from my base to my tip. This girl knows how to do magical things with her mouth and I will be able to experience it forever is, if she lets me.

She takes my bulging tip in her mouth and I let her give me a few good swirls with her tongue, before grabbing on to her hair pulling her off of me.

"As much as I would love to fuck your mouth, I have other plans. Sit all the way back." She does as I say, leaning against the wall next to her bed.

Her legs spread wide and I see her curls already glistening. I fucking love it that she isn't completely bare.

"Have you ever touched yourself while thinking about me?" I grab my cock and stroke myself, my eyes moving between her full breasts and her pussy.

Jordan surprises me by nodding. I raise an eyebrow. "When you first moved here. The morning that we went to breakfast." Her chest rises up and down, like she is trying really hard not to slide her hand down her body.

"And where did this little adventure happen?" I don't know just how much I can take before I have her on her back, but I will prolong this as long as I can.

"In the shower." She can't hold off any longer. Her hand starts to move to her chest, where I watch her play with her nipples before she moves it down until it's nearing her mound.

"Show me how you touched your pussy while you were thinking of me."

Being the good girl that she is, she runs her fingers against her mound and then she slides them along her folds. She teases her entrance before going up slightly and circling her clit.

"Do you want a taste?" She holds out her hand for me and I don't hesitate to climb onto the bed and take her wet fingers in between my lips.

The best fucking taste in the world.

Popping her fingers out of my mouth, I situate myself between her legs, putting each one over my shoulders and eating her out like she's my last meal.

"Fuck. Mason," she pants out, her fingers making their way to my hair and holding me to her.

I love the pain of her pulling my hair.

Humming against her, I insert two fingers into her and hips buck against them.

"You're so fucking tight. I can't wait to slide my cock in you, so you can wrap this tight pussy around it."

She lets out a loud moan that fills the room.

"More." She's on the edge of exploding around her fingers so I do a come hither motion. Within seconds, she tightens even more around me and coats my fingers with every last bit of her orgasm.

"That's it, baby." I lick up her release and she starts to come down from her high.

I kiss my way up her body, taking each one of her tits in my mouth and finally ended up with my lips against hers.

"You taste so good." I slide my tongue into her mouth, giving her a taste of herself.

We kiss for a good five glorious minutes, before she pushes me onto my back and straddles me. I like where this is going.

"Condom?" my question comes as she slides her slick pussy along my cock, coating it in whatever is leftover of her orgasm.

There should be one in my wallet, since I know we ran out the last time I slept over.

Jordan stops grinding herself on me, takes her bottom lip between her teeth and looks down at me, "Maybe we can go without it?

Go without it.

"Are you sure?"

Every time that we've had sex, we've used protection.

I know that we don't really need it. Jordan is on the pill and we've both taken tests just to make sure that we were being safe. Yet we still use a condom for the sole reason that neither of us are ready to have kids. A discussion we already talked about.

"If that is something that you're comfortable with. I've never gone with one."

She nods. "Neither have I. I'm sure. I want this experience with you."

My hands travel from her hips up to her neck bringer her lips closer to mine. "I will give you every single experience you want."

My tongue makes its way into her mouth and I try to savor every inch of her mouth.

I move my hands back down and I grab her by the hips, lifting her up slightly until she lowers her body on my, as slowly as she can.

"You're trying to torture me, aren't you?" I groan when she is fully seated.

"Maybe."

I want to kiss that smirk off.

Grabbing her hair and pulling her closer to me, my lips feather-like against hers. "You can torture me all you want. I'm yours, and you're fucking mine."

I pull her hair back farther and place open mouth kisses on her neck, marking her as mine for the whole fucking world to see.

"Move, baby." And move she does. Her body feels like heaven wrapped in all the right places. She is wrapped around my cock so tightly that I have to think of something else for a quick second to control myself.

Letting go of her hair, I move my hand back to her ass and my mouth to her tits. I ravage them, pull and bite at her nipples claiming them as mine like I'm claiming everything else.

Her ass fills my hands nicely and the way she is bouncing up and down my cock is what I will be using to beat off when she isn't around.

Our groans, moans and pants fill the room and not before long, I feel Jordan tightening around me.

"Let go, Jordan. Let go." And she does. I'm not far behind, pounding into her a few more times before I finally let myself explode and fill the condom.

"Fuck!"

Jordan falls onto my chest and I hold her body tightly to mine.

After a few minutes, I lay her on the bed next to me and head to the bathroom to get rid of the condom. I quickly make it back to the bed and cuddle into Jordan's body.

"Have I mentioned how much I love night classes?" I press my face against her neck.

"What?" She giggles and turns in my arms.

"I hated night classes at the beginning of the year, and you changed my mind." She gives me a beautiful smile, and

I give her one in return.

"Well, I'm glad I was able to change your opinion.

"Me too." She leans over and places a chaste kiss on my lips.

"I love you, Mason Hawke."

"I love you too."

"Forever?"

"Forever. Broken pieces and all."

CHAPTER THIRTY-THREE

Jordan

"Would you stop fidgeting?" I giggle at Mason's nervousness. You would think that the man was meeting the president of the United States or something, by the way that his leg is bouncing up and down.

"What if he doesn't like me?" I'm sorry but this is a man that is well over six feet and he's worried about someone not liking him? What's not to like?

"It's my dad. You already met him." We are currently at Charlotte Douglas International Airport, waiting for my dad to arrive from Germany.

After a little over a month, military doctors finally cleared my dad to fly home.

He's finally going to be home. After years of wishing that he would be here for good, he finally will be.

Now the only person that I will have to worry about is my brother.

In the last month, Aiden has been around a lot more and it has let Dylan and I, Alana too of course, to rebuild our relationship again. It's not perfect, and we still have a long way to go to finally feel like siblings, but it will get there. A large part of our childhoods were covered in the cloud that came with Aiden and me drinking our lives away. Now that cloud has just started to dissipate.

My big brother and I have a lot of making up to do to Dylan.

"Yeah, well meeting your dad over FaceTime, where he can't kill me with his bare hands, is a whole lot easier than meeting him in person." Mason hisses in my ear, well not really in my ear because the man is standing a good three feet away from me. He won't even touch me.

"He won't kill you with his bare hands, he'll just strangle you and then slowly let you breathe again and do it all over again." I give him my best stone cold face. The way his eyes bulge out, he thinks that I'm serious. "I'm kidding."

"Your dad is in fucking army, shit like that can happen."

He is taking this way too seriously.

"I see him!" Dylan points to the figure that is turning the corner and sure enough, it's Daniel Garza himself.

A smile forms on his face when he sees us. He lifts a hand to wave and Alana charges at him. Within seconds, she is right in front of him, jumping into his arms, wrapping her legs around his waist, planting kisses all over his face.

"Are they always like that?" Mason nods over to where my stepmom is mauling my dad.

"That's nothing. I'm sure that I will be walking in on them fucking like bunnies every time I go into the kitchen."

Not an image that I would like to have in my mind, thank you very much.

"Can you not say 'fucking like bunnies' when it comes to those two?" I cringe just saying the words.

"Can I move in a few months early? Please? Save me from this torture." Dylan holds up his hands in a praying gesture and gives me his best puppy dog eyes.

"Sorry my friend, not going to happen." I pat his cheeks to get my point across.

"Besides, me and your sister will be fucking like bunnies until you move in." Mason lets out a grunt when I smack my arm across his stomach. "It's true."

"Yeah, but he doesn't have to know that." I'm dealing with a man child.

I move my attention back to my parents, because that's what Alana is… my parent, and I see that Alana finally untangled herself from my dad and they make their way to us.

Dylan is the first one to go to him. My brother is the same height as my father and the second that his arms are around him, he loses it. Dylan would never voice it but the possibility of losing my dad, wrecked him. If we had lost him, I don't know what would have happened to Dylan and that's not something that I would like to think about.

I had no idea that tears sprung from my eyes until Mason wrapped an arm around me, and leaned over to wipe my face clean.

Dylan and my dad release each other and I meet my dad's gaze.

About a week after we received the news that my dad was alive, we were able to talk to him. That's when Alana told him everything that had happened with me, and my trip to the hospital.

Not only did I hear anger in his voice when I spoke to him, but I also heard disappointment. It all brought me back to when I was a teenager and I knew my father hated me.

The tears that had escaped my eyes when I saw him

with Dylan come out at a faster pace now. Moving around Dylan, my dad holds open his arms and I run to him.

"I'm sorry," I mutter out through the tears and his arms tighten around me.

"*Mi princesa*, you have nothing to be sorry about. You're here. I'm here. That's all that matters." I hug him tighter, because after everything that has been going on in my life, I really needed my dad at this moment, and I don't want to let him go. Eventually I do though, because it's someone else's turn to greet him.

Aiden.

He and Sara had gone back to Oahu about two weeks ago, but he flew in yesterday to be here for when Dad arrived. Not only was Aiden trying to build his relationship with me and Dylan, but he also said that he wanted to rebuild it with dad too.

He told me that just because he wasn't his biological father, it didn't mean that dad wasn't his real father. Daniel Garza raised him, loved him and made him the man that he was today. Because of that, he was going to do everything in his power to rebuild their relationship, even if it took them years.

I smiled when he said that and I'm smiling now as my father walks over to my brother, who has apprehension written all over his face. They look at each other for a long minute before they have arms wrapped around each other. For the first time in years, my father and brother are acting like father and son and it makes me so happy to see.

When they pull back from each other, I see that the two of them have tears in their eyes and that just causes me to cry even more.

"Well, this sure wasn't a welcome that I was expecting."

We all smile at his words but I lose the smile when he makes eye contact with the person next to me.

Mason.

Fuck, maybe he does have something to worry about, because right about now my dad looks like a very scary man.

Daniel forgets about everyone else and walks straight to my boyfriend, who steps back from me. Literally putting three feet between us.

"Mason."

"Mr. Garza." I swear I can hear Mason swallow from where I'm standing.

My dad continues to stand there all intimidating and shit before he finally breaks and gives Mason a smile, holding out his hand to him. "Thank you for taking good care of my little girl for me."

Mason looks down at his hand and clears his throat before he shakes my father's hand, "It's my pleasure. Dani is my family."

I can't help but smile when he calls me Dani. Every time he does, it does something to me, deep inside.

My dad nods and grabs the bags that he dropped when Alana attacked him and we make our way to the car. To head home.

As we walk to the car, I look at my family. I never thought that after everything that we have been through, everything that I have put them through, that we would be here. Altogether, moving to the next step in our lives.

A month ago, I felt so broken and unstable that I thought that I was never going to see the light again. Yet, here I am with Mason at my side, his hand in mine, my father and brothers a few feet ahead of me and I couldn't be happier.

The broken pieces inside of me are still there, and they will probably won't go away anytime soon, and I'm okay with that. I'm okay with it because it gives me time to work on myself and on my life and what I want out of it.

Mason is helping me with that. Every single day, he tells me that I'm not the broken girl that I think that I am, that he loves me and that he will be there always when things get tough.

Each time he says those words to me, my love for him grows stronger.

I've done some horrible things in my life, things that almost killed people, things that almost killed me. There will always be guilt for everything that I have done and have put my family through, and just like the broken pieces, I'm okay with them not going anywhere.

I have a family that loves me, friends that will stick with me through anything and a boyfriend that is my whole world.

Life will always be unexpected when it comes to me, and I will be strong enough to handle it.

I know I will.

Everything be damned.

EPILOGUE

There is a calmness that engulfs me and a part of me wishes I can bottle it up and take it everywhere I go.

You would figure that being in a cemetery wouldn't make you feel that way, but given what I'm here for, I do.

I walk over to the plot that was mapped out for me by the groundskeeper. He volunteered to show me where it was but I declined. I wanted to do this myself, which is why I also told my mom not to come when I told her my plan.

I'm able to find the plot easy enough and my chest feels slightly heavy when I read her headstone.

Elizabeth Garza
Beloved Wife,
Incredible Mother.
Amazing Daughter.
Forever Friend.
1980-2010

So many things in just a short life.

Kneeling down, I take the dead flowers that were in

vase next to her plot and replace them with the fresh ones that I brought.

This isn't the first time that I have come to her gravesite, but it is the first time that I'm here without Jordan.

In the four years that Jordan and I have been together, we have come to Wilmington to visit her mom's site every single month. Usually when we are here, I walk up with Jordan and then leave to give her some time to tell her mom all that has been going on with her life.

Now I guess it is my turn.

"You may be wondering where Jordan is, well I didn't tell her that I was coming. Otherwise, she would be ruining her own surprise." I take a deep breath trying to collect my thoughts. I've never spoken to someone like this and it's throwing me off a little.

"I already talked to Daniel, Alana and also your sons about this, but I also wanted to talk to you too. I love your daughter very much Mrs. Garza, and I'm going to ask her to marry me. I think that we are ready for that next step and hopefully I have your blessing to do it.

"I promise you that I will spend the rest of my life trying to show her that she is a beautiful woman inside and out and that I love every single piece of her, broken or not. I will protect her from herself and from the world if she lets me and I will always be by her side, that you can count on."

For the past four years, Jordan has been my everything.

After her dad came home, we went back to Duke to finish up our third year. That summer we road tripped to Chicago and then to California to visit our grandparents and even went to Oahu to visit Aiden and Sara. I don't think I had ever seen her so happy and full of joy until that summer and I loved every second of it.

When we went back to Durham, we started our last year at Duke, Dylan moved in with her, and we started preparing for what life brought to us next.

We both ended up applying to graduate school at Duke and getting in, so we weren't going to leave Durham anytime soon. Which worked out because I think she was scared to leave Dylan all on his own.

After we graduated, I moved in with the two of them since Lucy and Damon had found a place of their own in Raleigh, what with them getting engaged and all during graduation.

Gabe ended up meeting a girl and followed her to Texas. According to Lucy, it wasn't going to last and she was right because he ended coming up back a few months later.

As for Carter, he took a teaching position at a local school. He seems happy and Jordan says that he has a girlfriend but that he hasn't introduced her just yet, and that there's something suspicious about that. Oh the greatness of your girlfriend caring too much about her best friend's love life.

I look back at the tombstone and think of how this woman would be proud of the woman her daughter has become.

I know I am.

Jordan still feels guilty for everything that she did, and I know she has a long way to go before she forgives herself fully, but she will get there. It all takes time.

She hasn't had a drink in four years. The week that she went back to Duke, after her trip to the hospital, she found out that the school had a program that helped students battle addictions. With the program at school and with routine check in with her sponsor, she was able to build herself back up again.

She says that there still broken pieces within herself, but that they aren't a prominent piece of her life. According to her, she hasn't had a dark day and she has hope that it will stay that way.

Jordan is in a good place and I couldn't be prouder of the person that she has become. I know her parents, brother and friends feel the same way.

"I will take care of her, and love until I take my last breath, that I promise you." I press my fingers to my lips before placing them on the top of the stone.

With one last look, I go meet up with Jordan.

* * *

"So, we're having dinner with Carter?" Jordan gives me a questioning look, when I pull into Carter's driveway, well the driveway of my old house.

"No." I put the car in park and then once the engine is off, I climb out and head to Jordan's side to open the door for her.

"Then what are we doing here?" She steps out and the red floral summer dress she has on, makes my fucking mouth water. Her tits look amazing in it.

"You'll see," she huffs but she walks toward the house without another word.

We walk inside and she gives me another questionable look, I just wave for her to head to the kitchen and she goes.

"What are you up to Coach Hawke?" Her hands landed on her hip, looking at me all sternly.

I can't help but chuckle, it's adorable.

Coach Hawke, damn I will never get tired of hearing

that. After two seasons as a team manager for Duke's baseball team, I left the position when I graduated. When the head coach heard that I was staying at Duke for graduate school, he offered me an assistant coach position. After talking it over with Jordan, I took it.

The baseball field is where I'm supposed to be and this position feels right.

"Do you remember our first morning together in this house?" I walk over to her, placing my hands on her hips.

She nods, her face filled with suspicion.

"That morning, I so badly wanted to go to you and see what your skin felt like against mine. I thought that you were hot, right away and then I found out you were the girl Carter was talking about the night before and I became more curious." My hands move higher up her body, bringing her dress up as they go.

"I told you that you had nice panties and I made you laugh. I was like a kid on Christmas morning."

I can tell by the look on her face that she is confused by the way that this conversation is going.

It's time to hit that home run, Hawke.

"A lot has happened and changed since then, but the one thing that hasn't is that I want to be able to make you laugh, as much as I can. Forever, if possible."

I let go of her hip and pull out the ring that I've had in my possession for over a year.

Jordan lets out a gasp when she sees it. It's a simple band with an oval diamond sitting right in the middle. It's not much, but it fits Jordan perfectly.

I drop to my knee and I hold out the ring to her.

"Jordan Daniella Garza, let me be there for you. Let me be the one to help you repair any broken pieces that you

256

think need to be repaired. Let me love you and let me be at your side as long as you need me to be. Will you marry me?"

Her hand goes up to her mouth, before she drops it and gives me a smile. "Yes."

I slide the ring onto her finger and stand up, placing my hands on her face.

"Forever?" I ask her, my lips barely touching hers.

"Forever."

This beautifully broken girl is officially mine.

Forever mine.

Want more Jordan and Mason? Check out their Bonus Scene at www.jocelynesoto.com/bonus-content

PLAYLIST

If You Want Love - NF
How Could You Leave Us - NF
The Trauma and The Pleasure - Cameron Sanderson
Brush Fire - Gracie Abrams
Hold Me Like You Used To - Zoe Wees
Sad Forever - Lauv
Walked Through Hell - Anson Seabra
Broken - Jonah Kagen
Arcade - Duncan Laurance
Unstable - Justin Bieber, The Kid LAROI

ACKNOWLEDGEMENTS

I can tell you right now that Jordan and Mason did not go as planned.

Storytime! The idea for this book came to me in high school. For reference, I graduated high school in 2012, so this story has been cooking up for a while. Originally the story was supposed to take place with them in high school, but when I officially started writing this book, I changed it to college because it became too chaotic.

So many parts of the story were supposed to be different but in the end the characters wrote themselves and I just went a long for the ride.

Jordan was a challenge to write and I tried my hardest to get her story right. Writing someone who has something in their life that is as big as an addiction can be hard and I hope that I was able to do her character justice. She is strong and deserves all the love in the world and I hope you love her as much as I do.

Also totally not necessary, Mason was almost supposed to be Josh. It seemed too matchy matchy for me so I did a poll on my bookstagram and Mason was chosen my popular demand! So I changed the hero's name. It completely fits him, don't you think?

I totally wish I had a Mason in my life, if you know of any send them my way. Jk.

Now onto my thank yous.

Thank you to the lovely ladies at Book and Moods PR! Thank you for working with me and helping me promote this book!

To my lovely beta readers, Mirella and Yesi, thank you for taking the time out of your day to read this book it means the world to me.

To my amazing editor Ellie (My brother's editor), thank you for taking the time to help me edit this book!

Thank you to the readers for taking a chance on my stories and giving me the courage to continue to right.

Thank you all so much!

Now onto the next book!

PS! If you go to the next page, you will get a sneak peak at Vicious Union!

261

Turn the page to get read the prologue for Vicious Union, book 1 in the Flor De Muertos Series.

VICIOUS UNION PROLOGUE

LEO

A killer.

A drug dealer.

Above the law.

All things that have been used to describe the type of person that I am.

Is there truth to them? I want to say no, there isn't, but then I would be adding liar to the list.

There has been more blood on my hands than any normal person could comprehend.

I look at the body that is in front of me, being drained of all the blood, and try to find something within me to feel remorse.

There isn't remorse, or even guilt for what I did. All there is, is anger. Anger at the man that was once a friend but turned into a narc. Anger at myself for not seeing the signs sooner.

Anger at my father for turning me into this kind of man. A man that will kill his closest soldier because he was communicating with the DEA. A man that hates the life that he was born into.

A man that just wants some normalcy. That wants to

build a life outside of the cartel, outside of the drugs and the guns. A life away from it all.

Even with a body in front of me, I can't help but laugh at the thoughts running through my head.

I will never live a normal life, I will never be able to walk away from him.

I'm Leonardo Morales and my life belongs to the Muertos Cartel. To my father.

This will forever be my reign.

VICIOUS UNION IS OUT NOW

BOOKS BY JOCELYNE SOTO

<u>One Series</u>
One Life
One Love
One Day
One Chance
One for Me
One Marriage

<u>Flor De Muertos Series</u>
Vicious Union
Violent Attraction
Vindictive Blood

<u>Standalones</u>
Beautifully Broken
Worth Every Second
Powerful Deception
Fake Love
Salutis Meae

ABOUT THE AUTHOR

Jocelyne Soto is a writer born and raised in California. She started her writing journey in 2015 and in 2019 she published her first book. She is an independent author who loves discovering new authors on Goodreads and Amazon. She comes from a big Mexican family, and with it comes a love for all things family and food.

Jocelyne has a love for her mom's coffee and writing. In her free time, she can be found reading a romance novel off her iPad or somewhere in the black hole of YouTube.

Follow her website and on social media!
www.jocelynesoto.com

JOIN MY FACEBOOK GROUP

Join my ever-growing Facebook Group.

https://www.facebook.com/groups/jocelynesotobooks

NEWSLETTER

Sign up for my Newsletter!
You will get notified when there are new
releases to look out for, giveaways and more!

https://www.subscribepage.com/
authorjocelynesotonewsletter

www.ingramcontent.com/pod-product-compliance
Lightning Source LLC
Chambersburg PA
CBHW030144200726
48285CB00006BA/1886